"I think you want me, Moranti. And you know it."

Jake's smile curved higher. "Moranti, my inhibited dear, you may talk like the last virgin in twentieth-century America, but you kiss like a woman who not only wants to make love but needs to. Why fight it?"

"Because—"Toby looked at him coldly "—I have more sense than to get involved with you. You're my employer. I'm your employee. That's that!"

He paused and stared back at her. "Maybe you're right. Maybe you are too smart to get involved with me. Maybe. Because you are smart, Moranti. You're very smart."

If I'm so smart, she thought, her knees beginning to tremble, *how can you make me feel this way? If I'm so smart, why am I still here?*

Bethany Campbell, an English major, teacher and textbook consultant, calls her writing world her "hidey-hole," that marvelous place where true love always wins out. Her hobbies include writing poetry and thinking about that little scar on Harrison Ford's chin. She laughingly admits that her husband, who produces videos and writes comedy, approves of the first one only.

Books by Bethany Campbell

HARLEQUIN ROMANCE
2726—AFTER THE STARS FALL
2779—ONLY A WOMAN
2803—A THOUSAND ROSES
2815—SEA PROMISES
2852—THE LONG WAY HOME

HARLEQUIN INTRIGUE
65—PROS AND CONS

Don't miss any of our special offers. Write to us at the following address for information on our newest releases.

Harlequin Reader Service
901 Fuhrmann Blvd., P.O. Box 1397, Buffalo, NY 14240
Canadian address: P.O. Box 603,
Fort Erie, Ont. L2A 5X3

Heartland
Bethany Campbell

Harlequin Books

TORONTO • NEW YORK • LONDON
AMSTERDAM • PARIS • SYDNEY • HAMBURG
STOCKHOLM • ATHENS • TOKYO • MILAN

ISBN 0-373-02877-6

Harlequin Romance first edition December 1987

CHAPTER ONE

IT WAS MONDAY at Fantod Studios, which meant that the three older cartoonists Toby worked with were more locked into their eccentricities than usual. "Postweekend weirdness," she'd privately labeled it, knowing that Hank, the senior member, would be particularly restless. Hank had spent Sunday reluctantly entertaining his grandchildren. This meant he would be falsely ferocious and genuinely demanding all day.

"Toby! Look horrified!" Hank commanded from his drawing board.

Toby, wielding her pen at her own board, smiled in resignation, then tried to look horrified. She widened her dark eyes and put her hand against her black curls as if she were desperately trying to keep her sanity in place.

"*Too* horrified," Hank complained. "I need horror mixed with sadness. Like you've just learned your paycheck isn't coming through."

Obediently, Toby laid down her pen and pretended to sob into her hands. "How's this?" she asked, her voice muffled.

"Too sad," Hank grumbled. "Come on, Toby, half and half—fifty-fifty—equal parts horror and sadness."

"You can do it, Toby," commented Ralph, who was inking one of Hank's finished pencil drawings. "Pretend you just heard Jake Ulrick got married."

Toby pretended to bristle. All three older men knew of her hero worship of Jake Ulrick and teased her at every chance.

She had learned to live with it. She moved her hands from her face and stuck her tongue out at Ralph, who, undeterred, crossed his eyes and grimaced wildly. Nobody could grimace quite as wildly as Ralph. The fourth member of their drawing team, Lawrence, ignored them all. He was hunched over his drawing board roughing in the dialogue for the cartoon strip "Judge Jackson." As usual, he was chain-smoking and in his own world. He blocked out the group with the old show tunes that blasted through the earphones of his Walkman radio. His head bobbed up and down awkwardly to the sounds he alone heard.

Toby tried to look fifty percent horrified and fifty percent sad. Hank shook his head. "Come on, Toby, now you just look like you've stepped on a bug. I need a combination of horror and sadness. Do it for me, gorgeous."

Toby sighed impatiently. "Why don't you make your own faces?" she asked Hank. "Use your mirror." Like her, Hank had a mirror fastened to his drawing board, so when one of his characters demanded an unusual expression, he could mug and copy the facial muscles.

"Because I'm drawing a woman and I've got a mustache," Hank answered. "I can't see what my upper lip is doing."

"So shave it off," teased Toby, but she did her best to make a sadly horrified face for Hank to sketch.

"He doesn't dare shave," cracked Ralph, dipping his brush in India ink. "He'd be even uglier without the mustache—if you can imagine that."

"Ralph, you're a moron," Hank teased cheerfully.

"This job made me one," Ralph said with equal cheer.

On the bulletin board above Hank was a cartoon he had drawn of the four of them. It was captioned "The Funnies Factory," and showed all four artists chained to their drawing boards with manacles and leg irons. They were hunched and sweating—Hank with his handlebar mustache, Ralph with his substantial paunch and supply of junk food, Lawrence locked into his private world of music, and Toby, all long black curls and dark eyes, slavishly drawing and wearing a sweatshirt that said Jake Ulrick Fan Club—President.

For the past three years, since she was twenty-one and had finished art school, Toby had been part of the cartooning team. She'd had no trouble being accepted by the three men she labored beside day after day. She had practically grown up among them. Her father and mother, now retired to Florida, had worked in the same low-priced New Jersey studio, on the same comic strips, for three decades. They had met here. The family joke was that Morantis were born with pens in their hands and ink stains on their fingers.

"The fabulous four," Ralph called their cartooning corps. He often sketched them, caped and soaring above the chimneys of North Bergen, New Jersey. He drew Hank as the superhero Mustache Man; Lawrence, with his earphones as Muzak Man; himself, overweight and carrying a supply of cream-filled cupcakes, as Munchy Man; and Toby, batting her eyelashes, as Cartoon Cutie, the Scourge of Man's Concentration.

The four of them were a tightly knit unit who worked long hours to produce two venerable syndicated newspaper cartoon strips: "Judge Jackson" and "Dr. Dinsmore." The fifth member, aging Allen Caldwell, the writer, worked at home, and appeared in the studio only on Fridays to hand in a week's worth of story lines for the strips. He had written "Judge Jackson" and "Dr. Dinsmore" for almost thirty years, ever since their creator, Robert Fantod, had become rich enough to turn the whole enterprise over to his assistants and retire to Honolulu.

After Robert Fantod died, the rights to his strips passed to his children, who lived a life of ease in Hawaii and never touched pen to paper except to endorse their royalty checks. But Fantod's name was still signed to the strip, and Toby, Hank, Ralph, Lawrence and Allen were the invisible and nameless crew who kept the adventures of the judge and the doctor coming, day after day, week after week.

In truth, none of the four was excited by the strips. The artwork was realistic but unimaginative; no innovation was allowed, and all four members of the team had come to genially despise the leading characters. Hank called Dr. Dinsmore "Dr. Dimwit," and was tired of the lovable old medic's everlasting wisdom and helpfulness. Judge Jackson was a clone of Dr. Dinsmore, except he was eternally wise and helpful in matters legal rather than medical. Ralph had given the judge a nickname that couldn't be mentioned in mixed company. "I hate this self-righteous creep," he'd grumble, as he inked yet another of the judge's good deeds.

The three men had come grudgingly to accept the limitations of the strips. "It's steady work," Hank would rationalize. "It's an honest living—sort of."

Despite having practically grown up in Fantod Studio Toby refused to think of spending the rest of her life there drawing the doctor and the judge. Like all young cartoonists, she dreamed of having her own strip. She had been drawing "Taffy," a series about a high school girl and her friends, since she herself was in high school. And, like other aspiring cartoonists, she was finding the struggle for acceptance next to impossible to attain.

For each new comic strip that the newspapers syndicated, hundreds were rejected. Year after year, no matter how hard Toby worked to refine and polish her creation, "Taffy" was among the rejects.

Her parents had always encouraged her to draw—drawing in the Moranti household was as natural as breathing—but about the possibility of her own strip they were reticent. "The pressure's incredible. You'll live a happier life as an assistant, believe me." That was all her father would say.

Her co-workers were encouraging, but cautioned her about the odds. While Lawrence and Ralph thought

"Taffy" was cute, Hank made no bones about his dislike of the characters and the concept.

"You're good," he'd told her. "You're better than good. You've got your father's flair and your mother's precision. You should be working on a strip a lot better than the doctor or the judge. But this 'Taffy' thing—I don't know, Toby, to me it just doesn't make it. You're so full of life, but when you draw 'Taffy' you go wooden—it's like you're trying too hard. Look, kid, you can draw like crazy and you can copy anybody's style. What you should be doing is working on a strip that's more challenging than these old wheezers."

But Toby persisted and Hank only shook his head. What he said was true. She could copy anyone's style so skillfully only an expert eye could detect the difference. But that talent held a peculiar curse—she didn't want to copy anybody else. She wanted to create a strip of her own, a style of her own, an original stamp. So far, she had failed.

It was natural that she idolized Jake Ulrick. He was young, just over thirty. His strip, "Heartland," had reached saturation point, having been syndicated in over two thousand daily newspapers. "Heartland" was totally fresh, funny, dazzling, sensitive and surprising. It was by turns poignant and outrageous. Hank, who was not easily impressed, called it the best daily strip to come along in the last twenty-five years.

Jake Ulrick had done it brilliantly, was still doing it, and was doing it alone, with no assistant and in relative isolation. Nobody on the East Coast had met him.

"Heartland" chronicled the trials and misadventures of the citizens of a small Midwestern town—Bigalow Springs. It was one of the few strips in which people and animals actually talked with one another, and somehow Ulrick had introduced a militant kangaroo named Waltzing Matilda who had immigrated from Australia. Despite the unlikelihood of a kangaroo in the Midwest, Matilda had become the strip's focal point and most popular character.

Everybody who read a newspaper knew of Bigalow Springs and Waltzing Matilda. The first words spoken in offices and factories across the country frequently were, "Did you read 'Heartland' this morning?" But nobody knew much about Jake Ulrick, and Ulrick intended to keep it that way. Rumor whispered that he was a workaholic and almost a recluse, that he still lived in the small town of Zion Bluff, Nebraska, where he had grown up, and that he abhorred publicity.

Toby had a photograph of him, cut from the back cover of his first book, tacked to her bulletin board. Hank said he didn't even think it was Ulrick's photograph, insisting that the artist had hoaxed the public with an old picture of James Dean. In the photo, he stood solemnly, baseball cap in hand, beside a large, particularly stupid-looking holstein cow.

Toby wasn't sure if the man in the photograph was really Ulrick, but it fulfilled her fantasies so completely that she kept it pinned up beside her favorite "Heartland" strips. The picture showed a tall young man with thick golden hair and serious, deep-set eyes beneath dark brows. He had a full, sternly set mouth, high cheekbones and a slim, straight Scandinavian nose.

Toby, who was small and dark and vivaciously Italian, loved his nose irrationally. Her own was delicate and slightly aquiline; a perfectly acceptable nose. But she had decided the man in the picture had the most beautiful nose she'd ever seen, and when Ralph teased her too often about the picture and her idolization of Ulrick, she would merely say, "I admire the man's nose."

"She's been drawing Dr. Dimwit too long," Ralph would say. "She's cracked. She's developed a nose fetish." He began putting glasses with false noses on them in her desk drawers, and decorating the margins of her drawings with penciled noses, if she stepped out of the studio for a moment. He and Hank and Lawrence had given her a horrible yellow sweatshirt for Christmas with Nose Lovers Anonymous written across the chest. In defiance, she wore it often, and she was wearing it today.

"Toby," Hank said, "Look horrified again."

Toby gripped her pen more tightly and cast him a volatile glance. "I just looked horrified for you," she grumbled.

"Aw, come on—once more."

She tried to look properly horrified.

"No, no, no," Hank reprimanded. "That's the same look you gave me before. I need a different horrified look."

"How many ways are there to look horrified?" Toby asked. "This is my basic horrified-sad look."

"I'm working on a different panel now. Dr. Dimwit's just told this woman her appendix is inside out and now he has to console her. Look sick with horror, will you?"

"Hank, I wish you'd shave off your mustache," Toby laughed, shaking her head.

"Come on, Toby," wheedled Hank. "Just once more. Sick with horror."

Toby thought of the greasy cheeseburgers they ate every day at the corner diner and struggled to look sickly.

"Good enough," Hank said, sketching swiftly.

Suddenly Lawrence spoke.

Lawrence, secluded in his private world of radio, spoke so seldom he actually startled the others. His left hand had flown to his earphones. "Hey, everybody—quiet," he said in an odd voice.

"What's the matter?" Toby asked, apprehensive. When Lawrence used that tone it meant he had heard bad news.

He took off his headset and looked at the three of them. He stared at Toby the hardest. "Your man," he said, not blinking. "He's been in an accident."

"My man?" she asked, puzzled. Lawrence was making no sense. She didn't have a man. She never met any eligible men. She wasn't even bothering to look for one. She put in a nine-hour day five days a week at the Funnies Factory, and in her spare time she worked on "Taffy" and did a few free-lance illustrations for the local newspaper.

"Jake Ulrick," Lawrence said slowly, still watching her. "He's been hospitalized. A horseback riding accident. His condition's serious."

Toby could say nothing. Hank swore, then asked, "How serious?"

"Serious. That's all they said," Lawrence replied. "A horse trampled him. Concussion and extensive injuries to the right arm and hand."

"Hand?" Toby asked weakly. The room seemed to darken and contract around her. *His right hand,* she thought in panic—*his drawing hand.* It had to be a critical injury to make national radio. She glanced up at the meticulously drawn strips of "Heartland" on her bulletin board. She felt physically ill.

"Hand? That sounds sinister," Ralph said bleakly. They all sat a moment remembering Standford, the brilliant young assistant on the "Artie in the Army" strip. He'd injured his hand so badly in a car wreck he'd never drawn again.

"Jeez," Lawrence said, shaking his shaggy head. "I hope it's not bad. If it is, it could be the end of 'Heartland.' Goodbye, Bigalow Springs. Goodbye, Matilda."

"Maybe it's not so much," Ralph offered. Nervously, he opened a new package of cupcakes. "Radio always gets news first, but they get bare bones—no detail. Maybe it's not so bad."

But instinctively, with an intuition so strong it made her weak, Toby knew it was bad—very bad. The best cartoonist in the country was lying in a hospital somewhere, the cleverness of his creative hand in jeopardy.

This time she had no trouble looking sad and sick and horrified. If Jake Ulrick's brilliance was snuffed out, or even impaired, something bright and irreplaceable would disappear from the world. Somehow, she managed to keep drawing for the rest of the day, but she felt bereft, robbed of spirit. The usual Monday madness that permeated the Funnies Factory slipped away. Even Ralph kept silent.

HANK, A KIND MAN in spite of his surface cynicism, insisted on taking her to the Shamrock Bar after work and buying her wine spritzers.

"Better?" he asked, concern in his raspy voice.

"I guess," she shrugged, not really feeling better at all. "Why am I so sure that something really terrible has happened? So terrible he can't do the strip anymore?"

"I don't know, but I feel the same way," he said unhappily, watching her over the rim of his Bloody Mary. "I'm getting bad vibes on this. And we won't get much more information from the news. His people will put a lock on it—they'll know how he feels about it. But we'll find out tomorrow."

"How?" asked Toby, feeling more frustrated and helpless by the moment.

"Through the syndicate grapevine," he replied. "The public may not know. The syndicate has to—he's their biggest money-maker. They can't let that strip die. If he can't draw it, they'll find somebody else who can. He can still write the thing and come up with ideas. But he'll need to get an assistant to draw it. It's the only sensible answer."

"He's the best cartoonist working," Toby protested gloomily. "Who could draw the way he does? Nobody could replace him."

"Wrong, my Italian scallion," Hank muttered. "You could. You could draw for anybody. And that includes the amazing Ulrick."

She shook her head sadly. It was the most absurd idea she'd ever heard. The two drinks had made her feel hazy and slightly dizzy. Lawrence's earlier words haunted her: "Goodbye, Bigalow Springs. Goodbye, Matilda." She felt as if there had been a death in her family. She wanted only to hide in her apartment, go to bed early and pray the news in the morning would be better.

But in the morning, the news about Jake Ulrick was infinitely worse.

TOBY SAT by her drawing board, staring unseeing out the northern windows at the gray New Jersey sky. Hank told her as gently as he could, but there was no way he could make the news less than devastating. He had tugged first one side of his graying handlebar mustache, then the other.

"I called Dunbar at the Empire syndicate," he'd said, watching her closely, for Toby was a woman whose emotions always lay painfully close to the surface.

"Public news releases are going to be stopped till Ulrick's out of the hospital. Some woman he lives with in Zion Bluff is calling the shots. I don't know if she's a secretary or a family member or what. And he's not going to be out of the hospital for a good three weeks."

"Three weeks," she said, biting her lip and still staring out the window. "So how bad is it?"

"Bad," Hank admitted. "He was riding along the river. A timber rattlesnake struck at his horse. The horse went crazy. Didn't throw him, but fell. Ulrick didn't get clear of it. Bad concussion and his arm's broken just below the elbow. Worse—several wrist bones were broken. It's his drawing hand, all right. They're worried about nerve damage."

"Nerve damage," she said tonelessly. Unconsciously she flexed the fingers of her right hand, her trustworthy, skilled and valuable right hand. Never before had she appreciated its delicate and ingenious construction. Never before had she considered how her very identity centered on that hand. What would happen to a man like Jake Ulrick if such a tal-
~ ~d instrument was robbed of its movement? She began
~l sick again. Without wanting to, she glanced again at

the "Heartland" strips on her bulletin board. She observed for a long time the drawings, and then turned away.

"Will he draw again?" she asked at last, looking at Hank.

He didn't meet her eyes. "So far the doctors are saying probably not. Sorry, Toby."

Sorry, she thought—what a weak and silly word it was.

She sat, brooding and staring up at the "Heartland" strips. "Does he know that?" she asked softly.

"I don't think so," Hank replied, fiddling with the nib of his pen so he wouldn't have to look at her. "He's still under sedation. In addition to the hand injuries, the poor devil took a bad blow to the head. They won't be able to tell him for a couple of days."

"And then what?" she asked, her voice almost pleading, as if Hank were some oracle who could answer the most difficult of questions.

He shrugged his stooped shoulders, trying to regain his familiar cynicism. "Then the man is going to have to make some adjustments. Even if he gets back the use of that hand, it's going to take time. The syndicate wants to send an assistant to Nebraska. As soon as he's released."

"He'll hate that," she said darkly. One of the few things everyone in the business knew about Ulrick was that he was a lone wolf, fiercely independent, a phenomenal one-man concentrated force of work and talent.

"Well," Hank said, becoming gruff again, "he'll have to swallow his pride and accept it. He's like everybody else in the syndicate—he's got a contract. If he can produce the story lines and the gags, somebody else could take over the drawing."

"It wouldn't be the same," she objected, fighting back tears. "He's a perfectionist. He'd never tolerate it. And nobody could do it—not as well as he could."

Hank was silent. Lawrence, for once without his earphones, chain-smoked and watched her. Ralph watched, too, uncharacteristically quiet.

Ralph shifted his girth in his chair, and took a deep breath. "Listen, Toby, the syndicate's giving him three weeks, just on the chance the doctors are wrong. But if they aren't wrong, the syndicate will force an assistant down his throat whether he likes it or not. The word's already out they might be asking for applications. 'Heartland' is better off than most strips—Ulrick works so hard he's nine weeks ahead of it. That gives them plenty of time to find the right person."

"Nobody can replace him," Toby murmured. A painful band seemed to constrict her heart.

"The syndicate's got over two hundred assistants working," Ralph argued. "Somewhere, there's somebody that can do it—they'll just go on loan to him."

"I got a feeling," Lawrence said unhappily, snuffing out his cigarette, "it's going to be a permanent loan. The nerves go, the hand is gone. The hand is gone, the drawing's gone. He's going to need an assistant permanently."

"Yeah," Ralph added, "one who can do everything—rough art, finished art, inking and lettering. A jack-of-all-trades."

"Or a jill-of-all-trades," Hank mumbled, sketching absently. He didn't look at Toby.

"What's that supposed to mean?" she asked, her hurt suddenly edged with suspicion.

Hank kept his eyes on his drawing. "What I told you last night. You could do it. If they call for applications—and I'm sure they'll have to—I think you should apply."

"No," she said flatly. The news about Jake Ulrick was too depressing. She couldn't bring herself to capitalize on his misfortune. She would feel like a vulture.

Hank rose and walked over to her drawing board. He put one ink-stained finger under her chin and tilted her face up so s' had to look at him. "We talked it over before you   n—the three of us." He nodded at Lawrence and   'We think you can do it. I've told you a thousand times you should be going up in the world. Assist on a more challenging strip. This could be your chance to work on the best there is.''

"I couldn't," she said, trying to turn her face away. But Hank wouldn't let her.

"Listen, kid," he said gruffly. "You know you won't stay here forever. There are rumors already—the Morris Beechem people are interested in you. For the 'Family Fun-fare' strip."

Toby stared up at Hank, her dark eyes widening. Morris Beechem's strip of gentle family humor was a popular one. Like "Dr. Dinsmore" and "Judge Jackson" it was conservative and low-key, but its circulation was far greater.

"Me?" she asked, incredulous. "Work for Beechem?"

"Yeah." Hank nodded. "Only Beechem's tiring out and so are his ideas. You could do better. Go for the best. If they open up 'Heartland' to an assistant, apply. You owe it to yourself. You're young, you're fresh, you got talent and you got fire."

"And you know that strip and the characters by heart," Ralph added, unwrapping a candy bar. "You've studied it like it was a textbook. Think about it, Toby."

"I couldn't," she said, shaking her dark head.

Hank, in an uncharacteristic gesture of affection, put his hands on her unruly curls. "You owe it to yourself, kid. You might be just what he needs. Don't take this idolization thing too far. Ulrick's just a human being, like everybody else." He removed his hand, as if embarrassed by his display. "Everybody except Ralph, that is," he added with a growl.

Ralph only laughed. "Come on, Toby. The three of us put it to a vote before you came in this morning, and we all agree. You should go for it."

Lawrence nodded in shy agreement.

Toby was touched by their faith. She could tell from the charged atmosphere in the studio that the three men she'd known so long were serious. They were like uncles to her, members of her own family. But she couldn't think of applying to assist Ulrick. It seemed unthinkable, wrong, exploitative.

THREE WEEKS LATER, when Empire Features sent out a confidential memo that Jake Ulrick was out of the hospital and applications were being taken for an assistant, her co-workers had worn down her resistance. She finally agreed to submit a portfolio. Hank stayed after work with her for a full week, working until almost midnight, helping her polish and point the drawings.

"This is dynamite stuff," he said, late on the last night. "You're going to get it, Toby. You're going to do this."

"I don't know," she said. Her hand was tired, her eyes bleary, her confidence eroding.

"You'll do it," he repeated. He sounded tired but confident. "You got to. For us."

Surprised, she gave him a tired smile. "What do you mean?"

"You're one of us," he said with the familiar gruffness in his voice. "You have been since you were a little kid. You're going to do this for all of us—Ralph and Lawrence and me. It's practically like you're our adopted daughter. And you're going to break through to the big time—for us. Our girl makes good."

"Oh, Hank," she said, catching his hand to hers. "I don't know if I even want to leave you. This is too much like home. I'd miss you all too much."

He gave her hand a squeeze, then drew his own away quickly. "Everybody has to leave home, Toby," he said, his voice rasping. "Life means taking chances. Me—I never took the chances I should have. For you, I want it to be different."

He stood for a moment staring out the window into the darkness. Toby's heart tightened within her. She realized how fond she was of this gruff, kind, aging man.

"Just one thing," he counseled, his back still to her. "When you get it—and I know you will—don't be disappointed in the man himself."

She blinked in mild surprise. For a week they had spoken of the strip, its complexities, its techniques, its myriad subtleties. They had avoided talking of Jake Ulrick himself.

"I know he's your idol," Hank said in a low voice. "You think he hung the moon. But idols tend to have feet of clay. I get the impression he's a difficult guy, Toby. So you may be meeting a man with feet of clay—and a bunged-up right hand—and probably a lot of bitterness. It's not going to be like working here. It may be hard on you—very hard."

"Hey," she said, trying to change his suddenly somber mood. "I've worked with you for three years—do you drive us like slaves or do you drive us like slaves?"

He turned, and beneath his graying mustache his mouth curved in a sad smile. "This is different," was all he said. "This will be very different."

She nodded philosophically, but she was too fatigued for Hank's words to sink in. She could not realize at that point, late at night, in the old and familiar studio, how right Hank was. She did not begin to realize until the letter came from Empire Features telling her the job was hers.

"Dear Mr. Moranti," the letter had begun.

"*Mister* Moranti?" Toby had asked in amazed disbelief.

"It's a big syndicate," Hank had shrugged, unamused. "You think they know anything about us except that we put lines on paper?"

The letter continued:

We are pleased to inform you that Mr. Ulrick has selected you to serve as his assistant for an indefinite length of time. You are to fly to Omaha on Friday, June

20, Big Sky Airlines, flight 451. You will be met at Epley Airfield by Miss Cora Whitewater, who will drive you to Zion Bluff. Please wear a red carnation in your lapel so Miss Whitewater may identify you.

Miss Whitewater asks us to inform you of the following house and work rules:

1. The assistant is obliged to keep all information concerning Mr. Ulrick confidential. Violation of this stipulation will result in immediate termination.

2. This is a working relationship only; no entertainment will be provided. The assistant will invite no guests to Mr. Ulrick's home. Mr. Ulrick does not allow television on his premises. Discreet playing of the radio will be allowed, but only in the privacy of the assistant's room. The assistant may avail himself of the boating and horseback riding facilities.

3. After the first week, the assistant is responsible for his own transportation. The assistant will keep outside phone calls to a minimum.

4. Absolutely no smoking.

5. Drinking is to be kept to a minimum.

6. The work day will begin at 7 a.m. and continue until such time as Mr. Ulrick deems fit. Let the assistant be aware that Mr. Ulrick frequently works late into the evening hours.

7. The assistant will avoid making overtures of friendship or seeking confidences from employer and staff. Mr. Ulrick wishes an assistant, not a chum.

The only thing that made the letter vaguely tolerable was the salary, which was mentioned briskly at the end and made Toby's eyes widen. She was going into utter servitude and bondage, and it frightened her, but at least it paid well.

For a going-away present, Hank, Ralph and Lawrence gave her a blazing red T-shirt that said I Don't Want to Be

Your Chum. Toby packed it, but didn't intend to wear it. She knew instinctively that Jake Ulrick wouldn't find it funny.

When she departed for Nebraska, it was in true terror.

CHAPTER TWO

TOBY, FEELING SHAKY and slightly unreal, watched from the plane window as the hills and mountains of the east fell behind and the earth below her turned flat. Beneath her, the plains spread like a giant's crazy quilt in vivid shades of green, where only an occasional river stretched out, thin as an errant thread.

She nervously fingered the red carnation in the lapel of her red and white striped sundress. She was going to wear the petals off the thing before she reached Nebraska if she didn't stop fidgeting. She felt as if fate were whisking her off to an alien land, and her mind surged with unrest.

She worried that her work wouldn't please Ulrick. She worried that her personality would grate on him. She worried that she would hate Nebraska—Ralph had driven through it once and reported, grimly, that it went on forever and was nothing except corn, cattle and infinities of empty space.

She worried about Ulrick himself. How must he feel, she wondered, with his most brilliant gift snatched away from him by a freakish accident? Was he suffering pain, shock, grief? Would he resent her? Was he the kind of man bad fortune strengthened or the kind it broke? Would she be too awed by him even to speak, or would he be a disappointment, a rude and tyrannical taskmaster?

What would she do in her spare time, assuming he let her have any? She envisioned herself in a bleak farmhouse on a bleaker prairie, surrounded by miles of emptiness. From the road map back in her apartment, she could tell nothing about Zion Bluff except that it was tiny—less than a thousand people—and that it perched at the edge of the Missouri River about ninety miles from Omaha, the state's largest city. About Omaha she knew little more, except that it was a center for railroads, livestock markets and slaughterhouses. The knowledge gave her unpleasant images of diesel fumes and sausage factories.

Furthermore, she fretted, Ulrick was expecting a man and Hank had advised her against disabusing either Ulrick or the syndicate of the mistake. These were liberated times, but with Ulrick as set in his ways as he was, one never knew. He might be the type who thought a woman's place was in the kitchen, chopping logs for the wood stove, not capable of facing the grueling task of a daily cartoon strip.

Uneasily she plucked at the red carnation again. And who was Cora Whitewater, she wondered—relative, a secretary—possibly a mistress? She knew Jake Ulrick was a bachelor, but the name Cora Whitewater sounded intriguingly exotic. Toby imagined a leggy platinum blond, a rich rancher's daughter who rode a palomino stallion across the plains, the wind streaming through her hair.

When the plane began its descent into Omaha's Epley Airfield, Toby felt her heart drubbing against her ribs in panic. Numbly she slipped open her compact and examined her face. It was unnaturally pale. Her shoulder-length black curls seemed determined to be more unruly than usual, as if in sympathy with the chaos of her thoughts.

She studied her features critically. Would her very face offend Jake Ulrick? Hank always said she was pretty, but to herself, she looked dishearteningly ordinary. Dark brown eyes under feathery, slightly arched brows—the delicate aquiline nose that emphasized her Neapolitan heritage—cheeks slightly too round, chin slightly too pointed, mouth slightly too small—and tension straining every feature.

Relax, she commanded herself, and stared out the window at what she could see of Omaha. The sight surprised her. She glimpsed a surprisingly modern, large and spacious city, open and green, totally unlike the constricted urban complexes of the East.

The plane set down with a whoosh and a slight whump, then taxied to a standstill. Toby fiddled distractedly with her red carnation again, and another petal fell off. *Come on,* she told herself irritably. *You're from Jersey. Jersey girls are a breed apart. You can take anything these flatlanders throw at you.*

But to disguise her nervousness, she put on her oversized scarlet-rimmed sunglasses before deplaning. Besides, the Nebraska sunlight seemed unnaturally bright.

Inside the terminal, she stood with as much dignity as possible, wondering what Cora Whitewater's reaction would be when she realized only one person wearing a red carnation had got off the plane—and that person was the small and thoroughly feminine Toby. She imagined the tall and sun-gilded Miss Whitewater looking down at her, shaking her perfectly coiffed head, and murmuring, "This will never do."

She did not have to wait long. A blunt finger tapped her hard on the shoulder. "Not you," said a peculiarly resonant woman's voice. "Don't tell me it's you—are you Toby Moranti?"

Toby wheeled and looked into the eyes of a woman shorter than herself, but of sturdy build and coppery skin. The woman's eyes were blacker than Toby's, her straight hair even darker. It was blue-black, in fact, neatly parted in the center and hanging over her broad shoulders in two fat braids. She wore faded but expensive blue jeans, well-scuffed mocassins, a white silk shirt and a beaded necklace. She was somewhere between forty and sixty, and Toby realized with a start, the woman was an Indian.

Of course, Toby thought with slight shock—with a name like Whitewater, she should have guessed. But she stared at the woman in speechless surprise.

"I said," the woman asked bluntly, "are you Toby Moranti?"

Toby nodded, still unable to find words.

"Ha!" chortled Cora Whitewater, a wild half grin splitting her face. "Ha! This'll put a burr under his saddle—good! He needs it!"

"What burr? Whose saddle?" Toby asked, feeling herself slipping further from reality each second.

Cora gave a snort of laughter. "You. You're the burr. And you'll get under Jake's saddle. He's expecting some punk kid from Jersey who acts tough. Are you tough?"

"Only when I have to be," Toby answered, swallowing hard. That was true enough. She'd grown up as the only girl and youngest in a family of five children. Four hot-tempered and emotional brothers, even though they were frequently doting, had been devoted to teasing her, and she had learned the niceties of standing up for her rights.

"Good," Cora said, hitching up the belt of her aging jeans. "You'll need to be. You got a sense of humor?"

"I hope so," Toby replied, swallowing again.

"Good," Cora repeated. "You're going to need that, too. Now—where the devil do they kick the luggage out of the plane? I can't ever remember." She looked around in remarkable intensity until she spied the arrows pointing to the luggage-claim area. "There," she said, nodding briskly. "Let's get this show on the road." Hands in her hip pockets, she stalked off toward the luggage carousels, her thick braids flopping on her squared shoulders.

Toby clutched her purse and small red leather carry-on bag more tightly and scampered after her. Her red high-heeled sandals were new, and she felt as if she were hobbling in them.

"Come on, come on," Cora was muttering to the still-empty carousel when Toby caught up to her. "I haven't got all day. I got things to do."

Toby cleared her throat delicately. "Ah, just what exactly do you do for Mr. Ulrick?" she asked curiously.

"Everything," Cora replied shortly. She tapped her foot impatiently.

That covered a lot of territory, Toby thought ruefully. "How long—" she ventured at last "—have you worked for him?"

"Forever," Cora answered, with equal brevity, glowering at the nonappearance of the luggage.

Well, thought Toby, in books and movies American Indians were depicted as people of few words, but Cora Whitewater was taking laconic no comment to new lengths. "Just how long is forever?" she prodded, wishing the suitcases would arrive. Cora seemed ready to explode with restlessness.

Cora tossed her a brief black glance that was neither friendly nor unfriendly. "Since he was six. I raised that boy. Me and his granny. And it was some job, let me tell you."

Mercifully, the luggage began to roll into view. Toby was relieved to see her pair of crimson suitcases appear, along with the heavy black case that held her portable drawing board and art supplies. She reached for the drawing case, but Cora beat her to it.

"This is yours," she said, not questioning the fact at all. She set the case down with a resounding thump, then seized the two red suitcases as they moved by. "And these—" she met Toby's dark eyes with her startling direct ones "—these are yours, right?"

"Right," Toby admitted, feeling a bit startled by the woman's prescience. "How'd you know?"

Cora handed her the smaller suitcase, hoisted the larger two pieces effortlessly and began to half run, half sprint toward the parking lot. Toby followed as best she could on her unaccustomedly high heels.

"They had to be yours," the older woman reasoned, hardly turning her head. "Everything about you matches—red flower, red dress, red shoes. So it figures—red luggage. And everything looks new. You buy all this stuff new, just to come out here?"

Cora was already at the trunk of a low-slung vintage white Cadillac. Toby nodded reluctantly. Her wardrobe in New Jersey hadn't been extensive, and her luggage, an inheritance from her brother Tony, was a battered scandal. She had dug into her savings to make her entrance into Nebraska and the stronghold of Jake Ulrick fashionably respectable, if nothing else.

"Too bad," mused Cora, unlocking the trunk and heaving in the luggage without ceremony. "You know the saying about distrusting all occasions that require new clothes. You know who said that, don't you? Henry David Thoreau, that's who. The philosopher."

Toby hadn't known, and only watched as Cora took her carry-on bag and small suitcase and pitched them into the trunk.

Cora slammed the trunk shut with a violent flourish and opened the car doors. "I wanted to bring Jake's car, 'cause it's faster, but he won't let me touch it," she said, letting Toby in. "He says I drive crazy. Hmmph."

"This is a lovely car," Toby offered, eyeing the flawless blue interior of the Cadillac. "Is it yours?"

Cora nodded briskly, then fired up the engine. "Jake gave it to me the last time he was in a good mood. I think that was five years ago."

Mercy! thought Toby, madly fastening her seat belt as Cora careered out of the parking lot, squealing tires on the pavement. The woman drove as though she were in training for the Daytona Speedway.

On the open road, Cora threw back her head and laughed
again. "Ha!" she repeated. "Ha! A woman. This is rich.
You'll be staying in the house with us. I knew Jake would
rue the day he put that doctor in the guest house. This'll
teach him."

"What doctor?" Toby asked, watching the emerald
cornfields flash by at what felt like the speed of light.

"That doctor," Cora returned darkly. "You'll see. Boy,
will you ever see."

Toby settled back nervously. Cora was speeding, but her
hands on the wheel looked totally capable. Rings of silver
and turquoise flashed on her fingers. Toby was still in a
slight state of shock to find herself being carried off by an
Indian, complete with braids and beadwork. "Do you mind
if I ask you a question?" she asked at last, tentatively.

"I'm not supposed to answer questions," Cora said, her
face unreadable. "But it depends on the question. Maybe I
will and maybe I won't."

"Well," Toby said rather weakly. "Do you and Mr. Ulrick happen to be—er—related? Or something?"

"Related? Hardly!" the woman laughed. "Or does that
question mean, is he Indian, too? Think I'm taking you off
to the reservation? No. His people were Scandinavian. Mine
were a hundred percent Indian, but I prefer Native American. Some people call me a Sioux, but I prefer Lakota. It's
the real name of our nation. So I'd appreciate keeping the
terminology precise, okay?"

"Okay," Toby agreed, wanting to appear reasonable.
"Native American and Lakota it is. How about another
question?"

"I told you. I'm not supposed to talk much. Maybe I'll
answer and maybe I won't. Try me."

"Who says you're not supposed to talk—Mr. Ulrick?"

Cora stroked one of her thick braids. "Could be. I'm not
saying."

"Well," Toby tried again, rather lamely, "you've known him a long time. Would you say he's a difficult man to work for?"

"No," Cora answered, a carefully speculative look on her face. "He's not difficult. He's impossible. That scare you?"

"Certainly not," Toby lied. "The whole cartoon business is impossible. Why should one man scare me?"

Cora shrugged. "You'll see. Believe me."

"How's his hand?" Toby asked. It was a bold query, but the question had haunted her for weeks now.

"I can't talk about that," Cora answered tersely. "None of us talk about that. And whatever you do, don't ask him. Or I'll be driving you right back to that airport tomorrow."

They sat for a few moments in silence, Toby feeling uncomfortable, Cora looking both troubled and stubborn.

"How about some music?" the older woman asked at last, tossing Toby a look that was almost kindly.

"That'd be fine," she answered with relief.

Cora slid a cassette into the tape deck and within a few seconds the car was filled with the strains of a symphony by Mozart.

Cora hummed along with passion and Toby stared at her in surprise.

"What's the matter?" Cora asked, casting her a sideways glance. "You don't like classical?"

"Classical's fine, classical's great," Toby insisted, sorry she had stared. Any stereotypes or preconceptions about Native Americans she'd had were rapidly evaporating.

"Me," Cora said, almost smiling, "I like Mozart best—the music's got elegance—but joy, too. Listening to Mozart reminds me of the way Jake draws." Her broad face suddenly went sober. "Used to draw," she corrected herself after a moment. Then she added, "The way they both used to draw."

There was a beat of charged silence in the conversation.

"They both used to draw?" Toby asked, disturbed and puzzled. "Who's the other one—besides Mr. Ulrick?"

"I can't answer that," Cora said stonily. "I told you. I'm not supposed to talk."

But Toby felt a prickly certainty that Cora did want to talk, that she had wanted to talk to somebody for a long time, and that she needed to talk.

She sat in confused silence, watching the rolling jade-green fields flow past. Their impossible brilliance was matched and made more intense by the seemingly endless sweep of flawless blue sky. It was country unlike any she had seen or even imagined.

She suddenly felt a bit like Alice, falling through the rabbit hole and finding herself in Wonderland. Only instead of a Red Queen, a magical cat and a Mad Hatter, she was about to be living with a Lakota woman with a taste for Mozart, a mysterious doctor whose name she didn't even know and an artist who was not merely difficult, but impossible.

"Tell me," she said carefully, deciding to try one more question. "That picture on the back of his first book—was that really Mr. Ulrick?" She had fallen half in love with the sun-streaked hair and moody blue eyes of the man in the photo. She wanted to prepare herself for the disappointment if it proved not to be Ulrick after all.

Cora gave her an odd glance, then returned her gaze to the road. "No," she said dispassionately. "It isn't him."

"Oh," said Toby, her last illusion dashed.

"But it doesn't make any difference," Cora added mysteriously. "Because it might as well be."

She declined to say more. Toby thought uneasily once more of *Alice in Wonderland* and Alice's bewildered line: "Things are getting curiouser and curiouser." *Indeed they are,* she mused nervously. *Indeed they are.*

Nebraska, Toby quickly discovered, wasn't all flat. Cora drove northward, and the hills became increasingly frequent; they were verdant and strangely shaped, like something out of a slightly abstract painting. Cora, who volunteered little other information, said the formations had been left by the last glaciers, and besides, this was the eastern river country, not the western plains section.

Toby's heart gave a small lurch when they finally reached the town limits of Zion Bluff. It was a sleepy little place, its main street lined with false-fronted buildings that showed its frontier heritage. But Cora kept driving, and in a moment, Zion Bluff was behind them.

"We live in the country," Cora explained, seeing the puzzled look on Toby's face. "In the heart of the heart of the country, as some poet once said. On the river. On that damned robbing river."

The hills grew steeper, the cornfields less frequent, the trees thicker. The road turned to gravel, then to black dirt as it slanted up even more steeply. Maple, oak and scrub pine clustered more thickly.

Then at the crest of the wooded hill, there was a clearing, and in the clearing, a house such as Toby had never seen. It was half gray stone, half log, and looked like a cross between a frontier fort and a small castle. It even had a pair of stone turrets soaring into the blue sky. Behind it were a cluster of small but graceful log buildings, and then a bluff that dropped off sharply. Beyond she could see the broad and turbulent waters of the mighty Missouri River. What she had read of it was true—it was so muddy it looked like of a torrent of chocolate.

But as strange as the house and as eerily stirring as the tossing river were, Toby's attention was caught by two men on the broad and lushly green lawn. One, stiffly astride a small bay horse, was short, plump and balding, his head gleaming in the bright sunlight. The other looked altogether natural on a large splashy pinto that was spiritedly rearing and pawing at the perfect grass.

Its rider was a long-legged blond man in jeans. His thick golden hair was rumpled and it glinted in the afternoon light. He was half grinning, half grimacing at the antics of the brown and white horse as his left hand fumbled at the reins. With a shock she recognized him: Jake Ulrick—and he was the man in the picture. He had the same gilded hair, the same moody brows and strong, sensitive mouth. He even, she noted with the slightest lurch within, had the same straight and perfect nose. Why had Cora said he was not the man in the photo?

Then the horse wheeled, and she saw his right arm, immobile, a lightweight cast from wrist to elbow and a black glove covering his hand.

Cora squealed the Cadillac to a halt and was out the door before Toby could say a word. The older woman half ran, half strode to the riders, said something in obvious anger to the small, balding man, and something more angrily to Jake Ulrick, and seized the pinto's bridle.

Jake Ulrick raised his head and laughed into the sky, but Toby sensed bitterness in his laughter. Feeling dazed and dreamlike, she took off her sunglasses and stepped out of the car.

"What kind of fool stunt, anyway?" Cora was demanding, refusing to release the pinto's bridle. "You're not out of the hospital three weeks and now you're trying to galavant around on this crazy thing? You're not going riding, so get down."

"I've already been riding," Jake Ulrick laughed, his lip half curling in defiance. "You're too late—so just calm down, Cora. I'm not six years old any more."

"This horse nearly killed you once," Cora argued. "Now you want to let it finish the job?"

"It wasn't Tango's fault," Jake pointed out, keeping the restless horse under control. "If a rattlesnake popped out of the brush at you, you might jump up and fall over backward yourself."

"It's important that he resume normal activities," said the small man pompously. He had an undefinable accent that sounded vaguely English. "It's important not only physically but psychologically. Body and mind are intimately related. As my dear friend Swami Mahrami was fond of pointing out—"

"I'd like to put you and your friend the swami on this crazy horse," Cora snapped. "You may have a lot of college degrees, but you don't have the sense of a common-sized louse. What'll you have Jake doing next? Sitting on a flagpole?"

"Of course not," sniffed the small man. "Sitting on a flagpole is not what either his mind or body is accustomed to. Contain yourself, my good woman. You are interfering with the march of science."

Cora started to make an angry retort, but Jake cut her off abruptly. Across the lawn his eyes met Toby's staring ones. His gaze was an incredible piercing blue, hot as the sky behind him. Toby felt as if she were being riveted by laser beams.

"Who's that?" he demanded harshly, nodding in her direction.

"That's your assistant," Cora tossed back. "So why don't you get off this bronco and greet her? While you're still in one piece—more or less."

Wordlessly, still not taking his eyes from Toby, he tossed Cora the reins. Expertly, without using either hand, he swung one long leg over the cantle of the saddle and dismounted. He stood, his weight on one booted leg, his right arm hanging stiffly by his side. He put his left hand in the back pocket of his jeans. He stared at Toby until she felt guilty and somehow naked. She wished she had left her sunglasses on, so the power of that stare would be dimmed.

"That's a woman," Ulrick said at last in a low, disbelieving voice.

"Very good," Cora said sarcastically. "Go to the head of your class. And she seems like a nice woman. So try to act like a gentleman for once in your life."

"This is indeed a pleasure and a surprise," the small bald man piped up. Gingerly he began to dismount the bay, but the horse began dancing backward under his nervous movements, and he uttered, "Whoa! Whoa!" in a slightly alarmed voice.

Jake Ulrick still hadn't taken his hot and moody eyes from Toby. He began walking toward her, ignoring both Cora and the man Toby assumed to be the mysterious doctor. He stopped and looked Toby up—from the dark curls of her unruly bangs—and down—to her high-heeled red sandals.

"You're a woman," he repeated in the same accusing voice. His eyes came to rest again on her dark and apprehensive ones.

Toby kept her back straight. "Right," she said crisply. It was only one word, but she felt she'd got it out with sufficient self-confidence. Seeing the intense displeasure on his face, she wondered if he were going to dismiss her here and now.

Instead he looked her up and down again, then gazed off with disinterest into the trees. "Hell," he said at last. "I don't care if you're some sixth sex that came from Mars. Nobody else that applied could draw. You can't either, but from what you sent, you could be taught."

Toby stiffened even more. She was used to being teased, but not insulted. The man's insolence cut through her fear and stirred anger she fought to control.

"Well," she challenged, her voice low. "I'm here. So teach me."

"I'll teach you, all right," he asserted. "More than you ever wanted to learn. At the rate I'm paying you, I own you, body and soul. You're going to work like you never worked before in your life."

"Fine," Toby replied evenly. "I've always earned my pay. I'm not afraid of work."

"Stop trying to intimidate the girl, Jake," Cora said. "She's here to help, for heaven's sake."

Jake tossed Cora a disgusted look. "As if one woman in the house isn't enough. Just keep her out of my way when I'm not working."

Cora's strongly boned faced darkened with disapproval. "I don't know why she'd want to be in your way. You're no joy to be around, believe me. And if you don't want her in the house, move your friend here—" she gave a disdainful nod toward the doctor, who was now clambering down from the bay with a total lack of grace "—and let her have the guest house."

"That would be impossible," protested the little doctor, who was sweating profusely. "I was promised the guest house. I have my research to pursue, my meditation exercises, and I'm working on my neurosynchronization enrichment machine—I cannot move my equipment."

He walked toward Toby, extending a pudgy hand. She shook it and found it unpleasantly damp. "I am Dr. Wendell Hyde-Crippen," he said, stroking her knuckles with his plump thumb. "Were my work here not so important and my research on the enrichment machine at such a critical stage, nothing would give me greater pleasure than to relinquish the premises to so lovely a young lady. For a lovely young lady you are—Miss Moranti, is it? I have always found dark-eyed women particularly irresistible."

Then to Toby's surprise and slight revulsion, he raised her hand to his lips and kissed it. "I salute the beautiful hand that will assist our friend Mr. Ulrick as he travels the road to total recovery."

Cora stared at Dr. Hyde-Crippen with barely disguised loathing, but Jake Ulrick, catching her look, permitted himself an off-center and slightly bitter smile. He took the reins from her and started to lead the pinto away.

"Where do you think you're going?" Cora demanded, with a challenging squint.

"To rub Tango down. Shouldn't you go make supper or something? The lady in red over there is probably hungry."

He tossed Toby a brief, cold glance, then began leading the high-stepping pinto toward the largest of the log outbuildings.

"If you think you're going to rub that horse down with one hand—" Cora began, her voice edged.

"It is important that the old patterns and activities be reestablished as swiftly as possible," Dr Hyde-Crippen reminded her. "And kindly do not overcook my vegetables tonight, Miss Whitewater. You boil the most important nutrients completely out."

Cora glowered at the little man, but he ignored her, returned to the bay horse and began leading it toward the stable.

Cora put her hands on her hips and watched them go. Toby could tell she was fuming.

Cora looked over her shoulder and nodded toward the house. "Come on, kid," she said, her face grim. "I'll show you where your room is. Then you can join me in the kitchen for a cup of coffee. I don't know about you, but I need one."

In spite of Toby's wildly spinning emotions, she was impressed by her room, for it was both spacious and charming, with the fairy-talelike advantage of being in the top of one of the stone turrets. The room was almost completely round, with long windows that overlooked the river. Part of it was taken up by a small private bath, done in dusty pink and rose that echoed the rich colors of the carpet, satin spread and drapes of the main room. There was even a small marble fireplace, and on an antique table, a tiny black-and-white television.

"I thought," Toby said dubiously, "that Mr. Ulrick didn't allow television."

Cora set the suitcases briskly on the bed. "He doesn't. But you can't live like a hermit. I put it in here. If he doesn't like it, he can tell me about it. He and I have been arguing for twenty-four years, so what's one more fight?"

Cora looked lost in troubled thought for a moment, then shook her head so that her braids swung. "I guess you're a big enough girl to unpack by yourself. So when you're finished, come on down to the kitchen for coffee."

Cora left, and Toby heard her thunder down the stairs as if in an excess of impatient energy. Numbly she unpacked her things, wondering if she should change, but decided against it.

Fifteen minutes later she found her way to the huge and sunny kitchen where Cora's coffee filled the air with its tempting aroma.

"Sit, sit, sit," Cora ordered, waving Toby to a large oak table with claw feet. She set a pair of sturdy yellow mugs on the table and poured the coffee. With a massive sigh, she sat across from Toby and stared out the window toward the river.

Toby raised her mug and sipped. The coffee tasted like ambrosia. "This is wonderful," she said with a sigh of her own. She watched Cora, who seemed to be slipping rapidly into a dark mood. "I see what you mean about the doctor," Toby offered shyly. "He's a bit—unusual."

Cora turned her frank gaze to the younger woman. "Unusual is a polite way to put it. I put it another way. I can tell you with a riddle."

"A riddle?" Toby asked. How many mysteries clustered in this beautiful but hostile house?

"Yeah," Cora replied, her eyes still holding Toby's wondering ones. "What's a duck say?"

Toby blinked in surprise. "A duck says—quack." she replied, not understanding.

Cora nodded grimly. "Right. And that's what that Hyde-Crippen is—a quack. Quack, quack, quack. He was probably born in the mouth of ducks—damn him."

"Then," Toby asked, perplexed, "what's he doing here?"

Cora stared gloomily into her coffee cup. "He's here because he's the only one who tells Jake what Jake wants to hear—that he'll cure that hand. There are three other doctors who say no, and one who says there's an outside chance. But the quack says different, and so the quack's here. If Jake wasn't so desperate, he'd see right through him. Jake's always been stubborn. But he's never been stupid. Until Hyde-Crippen. Hyde-Crippen—pah!"

Toby sat in shock, watching Cora's strong, brooding face. There were tears in the older woman's black eyes, and for the first time Toby realized how complex and difficult the situation was going to be.

Brusquely Cora brushed the tears away with the back of her hand. "Anyway," she said, "I'm glad you're here. Maybe you'll help. Heaven knows something has to."

She rose, leaving her coffee mug half full. She went to the counter and stared out at the bluffs.

"This isn't a happy house," Cora said, her back straight. "Except I do love Jake. There's that left, at least. But just when I thought we were getting our lives in order at last, this happened."

She crossed her arms over her breasts and turned to face Toby. "Look," she said, "he didn't want an assistant and he wasn't expecting a woman. He tried to intimidate you, and he'll keep on trying. What you've got to understand is the things Jake loves most are imaginary—and created by his own hand. Now the hand won't work. He'll have to use yours. He resents that, kid. He might even hate you for it. But it's not really you he hates. It's having to need somebody."

At that moment the back door crashed open, and Jake stalked through the kitchen. When he entered, he filled the room with something like electricity. It left Toby both frightened and breathless. With his left hand he gave Cora a swat on her jeaned behind, a gesture of gruff affection. "The doctor wants his vegetables and brown rice," he muttered. "He wants them now."

"Vegetables," Cora practically sneered, but Jake continued on his way and disappeared through the door into the dining room. He hadn't bothered to glance at Toby, yet his impact on her was devastating.

He hates me already, she thought in despair. Yet her heart tightened in reluctant compassion for him. He was like a force of nature—unconquerable, proud, untamed and untamable.

Cora, still moody, seemed to read her thoughts. "Oh, yeah," she said between clenched teeth. "He's got his courage left. He's always had more than his share of that. There's only one kind of courage he doesn't have."

"What's that?" Toby asked softly.

Cora shrugged, her face implacable. "The courage to give up," she muttered tonelessly. She bent over the vegetables, beginning to scrub them furiously, and Toby thought she saw the glint of tears in her eyes again. "He just doesn't know how to give up. He never did. Heaven help him."

CHAPTER THREE

TOBY AND CORA ATE a light supper together. Dr. Hyde-Crippen, it seemed, usually dined on his vegetables and brown rice in the solitude of the guest house, the better to digest his food and the day's experiments. Jake Ulrick ate when he felt like it, and lately, because of disputes over the doctor, he most decidedly didn't feel like eating with Cora. He took his meals in his room.

"Tonight he's avoiding you, too," Cora said darkly. "Trying to show you your place. His granny should have spanked him more when he was growing up."

Toby sliced a piece of cold chicken and gave Cora a measuring look. She was beginning to like the blunt woman. "You helped raise him. Why didn't you spank him more?" she asked. The atmosphere of the house crackled with disagreements, but somehow here in the kitchen she felt safe, even at home with Cora.

"Spank him? Ha! I should have," retorted Cora. "But I never laid a hand on him. You can blame my Lakota blood for that. My people don't believe in striking children. And you can see where that got me. If I had it to do over, I'd spank him till my hand fell off. The other one was never any trouble, but Jake—drove me crazy then—he drives me crazy now."

Toby studied Cora's bronzed and frowning face. "What other one?" she asked carefully. "Who was never any trouble?"

Cora shook her head. "Just the other one. Once there were two. Now there's just Jacob. We don't talk about it. Raynor's dead—ten years now. *Hechetu aloh*."

Toby realized she had pushed too far, but the strange words intrigued her. *"Hechetu aloh?"* she repeated.

"That's Lakota for 'So be it,'" Cora said stolidly. "That's about all there's to be said lately. And I find myself saying it a lot."

Later, in her room in the tower, Toby put her pillows against the brass headboard and leaned back, sketching desultorily. She halfheartedly tried to work on "Taffy," but her pencil seemed to have an evil spell on it. Nothing came out right.

Her mind kept returning to the day's uncomfortable events. Jake, as she had feared, neither welcomed nor accepted her. He was as handsome as she'd envisioned him, but more hostile than she could have imagined. She couldn't even bring herself to blame him for his hostility. He was a brilliant and talented man who would never draw again. Yet despite his brilliance, he had fallen into the delusive snares of Dr. Hyde-Crippen. Cora distrusted the doctor, and from the little Toby had seen of him, she disliked him herself. The pompous man, and the false hopes he so temptingly represented, could only make a difficult situation worse.

But more intriguing than the present were Cora's guarded remarks about a past that Jake seemed determined to keep secret—from Toby and from the world. Twice Cora had mentioned "the other one." She spoke as if she'd helped Jake's grandmother raise two boys, and one was ten years dead. The only logical conclusion Toby could reach was that Jake Ulrick had had a brother who died—Raynor. And if the photo on the back of the book wasn't Jake but, as Cora said, "might as well be," then the jacket picture must be of Raynor. In that case, Jake and Raynor resembled each other to the point of eeriness. Twins? It seemed a logical answer. The loss of the use of his drawing hand had not been Jake's first loss. There was the brother who was not to be mentioned, and besides that, since he had been raised by Cora and his grandmother, what had happened to his parents?

"Heartland" was a comic strip, full of jokes, full of fun, full of laughter. But the laughter, she feared, found its source in defying the darker corners of human existence. In spite of being as blond and gifted as Apollo, Jake Ulrick bore himself as a man who contained uncharted seas of darkness.

SHE AROSE, unrested and uneasy at six. She dressed demurely, in khaki slacks and a neutral cotton pullover, as if muted clothing would help her disappear into the background. She tried to do justice to the huge farm-style breakfast Cora set before her in the kitchen, but could not.

Her stomach knotted with anxiety as she entered the studio, the large, northernmost room in the house's lower story. She carried her heavy drawing case, and it seemed as uncomforting as a tombstone beneath her arm. Jake Ulrick stood waiting by the glass north wall of the room as she nervously eased herself through the door. She swallowed, although she knew she was not late. She was in fact five minutes early.

But he looked as displeased as if she were tardy by an hour. He wore blue jeans, black snakeskin boots and an old black sweatshirt with the arms torn off. The muscles of his upper arms were deeply tanned and latent with power. In contrast, the cast on his lower arm gleamed whitely in the morning sun. Toby tried not to look at the black-gloved hand, which struck her as sinister.

There was the faintest whiff of horsey aroma in the big room. Cora had grumbled that she suspected Jake had been up at dawn, secretly taking the big pinto for a gallop along the bluffs. Toby had no doubt that she was right.

Again, without wanting to, she was struck by the intense blue of his eyes, the challenging set of his mouth. His thick sun-streaked hair was rumpled, as if he had been raking the fingers of his good hand through it with impatience. The high cheekbones gave his face an austerity that was at odds with the disturbing sensuality of his lips.

She set her case down on a large antique library table and began to unpack her things. She moved quickly and with a competence she did not feel. Since he hadn't spoken, she decided to open the conversation herself, simply so he wouldn't think she was intimidated.

"Good morning," she said briskly.

He didn't bother to answer. He simply watched her. It was like being watched by some streamlined golden bird of prey. So he wasn't talking, was he? She could feel the resentful turbulence radiating from him. She could understand his bitterness, but she couldn't afford to feel menaced by it.

She looked at him with counterfeit coolness. "What do you want me to do first?" she asked, as businesslike as possible.

His blue eyes drilled into her so hotly they stung. She fought to keep from flinching. "Be quiet and wait for orders," he practically snapped, then turned his back on her.

Momentarily subdued, she stared down in humiliation at the table. But as the seconds of silence stretched into minutes, she felt her face growing hot with resentment. She knew he must hate having her there. He must be smoldering that the syndicate had forced her upon him. He probably felt she was capitalizing on his dilemma, eager to make her way up the ladder by leaping on the empty rung left by his accident. But did he have to be so openly rude about it?

He looked out the window as if infinitely bored. He looked for three entire minutes. Toby knew because she kept glancing surreptitiously at her watch. She struggled to stay calm as she set up her ancient drawing board. She heard him moving, rustling among papers at another table, but she refused him the satisfaction of looking up.

She felt him coming up behind her, like a palpable force of energy, as he impatiently thrust a heap of large sheets onto her worktable. She kept her dark eyes downcast, her mouth stubbornly set. Her sympathy for him—for she felt enormous sympathy—warred with an equally strong impulse to fling a bottle of India ink at his blond head.

At precisely seven o'clock, he deigned to speak again. "Don't come early any more," he ordered. "I told you—the workday begins at seven. And don't come late. Obey my orders exactly. I told you before—as long as you're here, consider yourself owned."

Toby didn't like being domineered. "Aye, aye, sir," she said with the false humility whose cutting edge was sarcasm.

"And don't be sarcastic," he warned. "You'll find I'm much better at it than you. Start by going through those rough sketches on the left. There's a week's rough art of strips. I want two days' worth done by lunchtime. I want the six regular strips finished by tonight and the Sunday strip roughed out."

She winced. She was nervous, her finger muscles already taut. Six finished strips in one day? The man either expected miracles or he was trying to drive her off on the first day.

Grimly she picked up her blue pencil and moved to the glass light table to resketch and refine the rough artwork. He followed her and stood, staring over her shoulder as she fastened the blank sheet over the first of the rough sheets. He worked with a different size of sketch than what she was used to—larger, which would make it harder. Her lines would have to be bolder, her work uncharacteristically oversized. Edgily, because he was still standing behind her, she began tracing the rough art. She immediately made a mistake.

She heard the displeased exhalation of his breath, almost felt it flutter the curls at her nape. Then he was bending over behind her, his good hand on the back of her chair, staring critically over her shoulder.

"Look," she said desperately, turning to face him. She wished she hadn't. His face was altogether too close to hers, and the force of those disapproving eyes nearly jolted her out of his chair. "Look," she repeated as calmly as she could, "do you have to lurk over me like that? You make it hard to concentrate."

With a gesture that startled and alarmed her, he put his left hand firmly on the back of her neck and forced her to face the light table again. Nor did he move his hand. It remained, hot, strong and commanding, tangled in her dark curls.

"You're going to need all the help you can get, Rembrandt," he said shortly. "Just draw. I'll 'lurk.' You'll see why."

"Then move your hand," she ordered, for his touch was sending alarm signals racing through her bloodstream. To her surprise, and wholly irrational disappointment, he complied.

"Don't know how you work with all that hair hanging around your face," he grumbled. "Can't you pull it back or something? You remind me of a sheepdog. How do you see?"

Steady, she warned herself, but this time he had actually made her truly and unadulteratedly angry. She gripped her pencil more tightly and glowered down at the roughs on the light table.

She sensed him reaching to the worktable. He tossed a fat rubber band down beside the drawing she was to trace. Then his hand was on her hair again gathering the thick curls together at the back of her neck. "Put the rubber band on," he ordered. "Get this mane fastened out of your way."

"I can see perfectly fine with it loose," she nearly hissed. "It doesn't bother me."

"It bothers me," he shot back. "Put it on."

With a fretful gesture, she put down her pencil, picked up the band and slipped it over the wealth of captive dark hair. Her fingers brushed against his strongly boned hand, and the sensation made her nerve ends freeze and scald at the same time. "Now let go," she said in perplexity, and she knew her discomposure had as much to do with the effects of his touch as it did with his overwhelming arrogance.

He gave the makeshift ponytail a light tug that was almost playful, then stepped back so he could see her from the side.

"Better," he said brusquely. "You've got a decent profile. Almost classic. If I have to look at you, I might as well see something worth looking at. But the perfume's got to go. It's distracting. Take a shower at lunch break."

She turned, staring at him in exasperated disbelief. "This happens to be very good perfume. And I like it." It was good perfume, she had bought it especially for the trip, and it had cost her an amount she didn't even like to recall.

"I said it was distracting. This is my studio and I don't like to be distracted."

"Me either," grumbled Toby, turning back to the light table. "Maybe you should take a shower at lunch yourself. At least I don't smell like a horse. You do."

He gave a short humorless laugh. "I can smell like a polecat if I want. I'm in charge here. Draw, will you?"

You can obviously act like a polecat, too, Toby fumed, but out of the corner of her eye she glimpsed his white cast, his black glove, and unbidden, her sympathies came surging back. She picked up her pencil and began to trace. She'd please him, she vowed, if it killed her.

SOON SHE WAS SURE it would kill her, because the man could not be pleased. The conversation had been one-sided, and it had all been negative.

"Not that way!" he criticized angrily.

"Look what you're doing, Moranti."

"What kind of shading do you call that?"

"Matilda's a kangaroo, Moranti, not a possum. Make that tail thicker."

"Sharper highlights in those eyes. I use the old-fashioned 'pie-slice' highlights, in case you haven't noticed."

"You're holding the pencil wrong."

"You're holding the pen wrong."

"Who in hell taught you to erase?"

She kept her mouth shut and willed her blood pressure to go down. Her only moments of peace came at ten o'clock when Dr. Hyde-Crippen appeared brightly at the studio door. "Cheerio! And hallo to you, too, Miss Moranti," he chirped in his affected accent. "Are we ready for our mid-morning therapy session, Ulrick?"

Jake replied with a curt nod, rubbing the muscles of his upper right arm. Toby, at work on the second strip at the light table, almost sagged in relief.

"And how's the pretty little assistant working out for us?" the doctor asked unctuously.

"She'll have to do," Jake replied in gloomy resignation. "If I had six months, I could teach her to draw. Too bad she isn't staying that long."

"Too bad indeed, too bad indeed," caroled the doctor. "But until I have you well, you must think of her literally as your right-hand girl." He sniggered at his own joke. Jake didn't laugh. Neither did Toby.

"Come on," Jake muttered to the doctor. "Let the torture begin. What's it today? Those damned deep muscle massages and weights?"

"This session I manipulate your spine again," the doctor said with great dignity. "We will be working on your *kundalini* force in general and your *mudras* in particular. Acupressure and electrotherapy at twelve-thirty, as usual."

"Right." Jake nodded without apparent enthusiasm. He turned to Toby. "Keep drawing. I'll be back in forty-five minutes."

"Miss Moranti looks tense—and tired. Pity, so early in the morning. Perhaps I should give you a massage after supper, my dear?" He flexed his pudgy fingers and gave her a friendly leer.

"No thanks," she said crisply, straightening her aching back. She vowed to have the finished pencil sketches done, and done perfectly, by the time Jake got back. Without him hovering over her like some angry god of perfectionism, she might be able to work at a decent pace. She drew until her wrist ached with the effort of absolute control.

Jake, his forehead and arm muscles covered with a sheen of sweat, stalked back into the studio exactly forty-five minutes later. He took one look at the completed strip sheet, shook his head, then growled, "You're going to have to do most of that over."

By lunchtime, she still hadn't done the pencil sketches to his liking, and it was a replay of the morning's critical bombardment.

"You've screwed up the spacing by a sixteenth of an inch there. What's the matter with your eye?"

"What in the name of all that's holy have you done to Swen Knudtson's elbow? Did a horse fall on *him*?"

"Matilda's not supposed to be just sweating in this close-up—she's sweating bullets, dammit. This isn't 'Dr. Dinsmore'—more comedy—more exaggeration. Follow the rough art, can't you?"

He worked her, correcting her incessantly, until twelve-fifteen, when Cora began to bang unceremoniously on the studio door. "Jake! Let her out! Lunch has been ready for fifteen minutes. The girl has to eat, you maniac."

"The girl can eat in fifteen minutes," Jake shouted back angrily. "We're already behind."

Toby, emotionally exhausted, heard Cora stamp away muttering to herself.

"I wanted these inked by noon," Jake said accusingly.

"So I'll skip lunch," Toby replied, fighting down the urge to scream the words. "I'll just keep working."

"The devil you will," he contradicted. "I've already seen the mess you can get into inking by yourself. You need constant supervision. And your knuckles are white and your hand is starting to shake. You need a break. You don't have any endurance at all."

Toby sighed in exasperation and ran a hand through her black bangs. She didn't trust herself to answer him.

When the plump doctor came at precisely twelve-thirty to spirit Jake away, she felt as if she had just been saved, as in a Western movie, by the appearance of the cavalry.

When Jake shut the door behind him, she switched off the light beneath the glass surface of the light table and laid her head down, frustrated and spent. Pain throbbed in her shoulders and neck.

She was still slumped over the table, her face buried in her crossed arms, when Cora found her and forced her to go to the kitchen and try to eat. There was a tray of delicious-looking club sandwiches and deviled eggs, fresh-brewed coffee, and homegrown strawberries, but Toby could only nibble.

"Bad, eh?" Cora said, leaning her cheek on her fist and watching her.

"Horrible," Toby said wearily. She stared with faint desire at a deviled egg, but it seemed large as an ostrich egg—far too large to pick up and actually eat.

"Umm," Cora said, her tone meditative. "Merely horrible. And you're not even crying or screaming. You may just work out, kid."

"Not to hear Mr. Ulrick tell it," Toby said bitterly. "He doesn't like anything I do. He doesn't even like the way I look." She touched her makeshift ponytail with distaste. "He even hates the way I smell. I'm supposed to take a shower before I get back to work—if I can crawl up the stairs and find the strength to turn on the faucets. How long do I get for lunch, anyway?''

"Cheer up," Cora said sardonically. "A whole hour. That weird doctor keeps him out of circulation until one-thirty, then he takes him off again at three for another hour. Then again at six. I don't know what kind of mumbo-jumbo he's doing, but it takes a lot of time—I'm sure you'll be delighted to hear. Give you a chance to get your bearings.''

"I think I lost my bearings permanently at about ten this morning," Toby said, rubbing her shoulders, "when he asked me if my head was made of wood.''

"Well, if you aren't going to eat, go up and take your shower. You got time to lie down for a few minutes. And I'll leave you something for your hair better than that rubber band. I forgot he doesn't like women with their hair long and loose. It reminds him of Denise.''

"Denise?" Toby asked, a barely suppressed wail in her voice. "Who's Denise and what's her hair got to do with me?''

"Sorry," Cora said, clearing the table. "Denise is something that we, well—''

"We don't talk about," Toby finished for her. "I'm beginning to see the pattern. Cora, you always drop a hint and then quit talking. Are you ever going to tell me the complete story about what's going on around here?''

"Maybe." Cora looked impassive and shrugged her broad shoulders. Today she was wearing a shirt of bright pink silk and a beaded necklace with a pendant depicting a thunderbird. "If you stick around here long enough. Think you will?''

For the first time that day, Toby almost smiled. "I don't know. Do you think I will?''

"I don't know," Cora challenged. "See, me?—I'm Lakota. I came from a nation of great warriors—naturally I can put up with somebody like Jake. Are your people noted for not backing off from a challenge?''

"Well," Toby offered. "At one point they conquered most of the known world. I mean, there was the Roman Empire."

"Which, as I recall," Cora said, her mouth quirked humorously, "got a lot of trouble from the northern barbarians—including the Scandinavians. Those are Jake's ancestors—the Vikings. We've got ourselves quite an ethnic mix here. We'll have to see who's fittest to survive on this battlefield. Go take your shower, gladiator. The blond marauder is due back in exactly thirty-two minutes."

Toby came blissfully back to life under the stinging spray of the shower. She bound her damp hair back with a beaded hair clip of Indian design that Cora had left on her dresser. She synchronized her watch with the digital clock on the bureau and timed her descent to the studio so she entered at precisely one-thirty. She timed it almost too perfectly. She and Jake appeared from opposite ends of the hall at the same moment, reached for the doorknob at the same time, and when their fingers brushed, both pulled back their hands as if they'd been stung.

He glowered at her, reached out again and swung the door open. "You smell better," he said, looking down at her still moist and curling dark hair.

"So do you," she said, her nose in the air as she sailed into the studio. He, too, must have showered, for his own blond waves were darkened by water, and he had changed the horsey-smelling black sweatshirt for a blue one, similarly aged and sleeveless.

Drat, she thought, her skin tingling. The blue shirt made his eyes as vivid as the northern lights. He ought to be forbidden by law to wear blue. It set off not only his eyes, but also his tan and the rich argent of his hair. He could probably walk down a street and kill women with weak hearts. If he'd ever bother to smile, he could kill women with strong hearts.

By midafternoon, she couldn't have cared if he were more handsome than Balder, the most beautiful of the Norse gods. She hated him. She loathed him. She despised him. And once, when he went hotly on and on about the trouble she had executing those difficult highlights in the characters' eyes, she found herself wishing hatefully that he had broken his neck, not his arm, when Tango fell on him.

The only respite she had was when Dr. Hyde-Crippen appeared to summon Jake to whatever peculiar ministrations were being practiced. Alone, she worked furiously. When he returned, he made her redraw half of what she had done.

They worked through the supper hour, although Cora's banging on the door sounded positively dangerous. At last Jake let her go, for half an hour, at eight o'clock to eat. Cora slammed around the kitchen muttering dire things about slave drivers, and Toby was dismayed to find that Dr. Hyde-Crippen had elected to wait and have his brown rice and lentils with her.

He told her she had lovely skin and glossy hair, but would be even more radiant if she followed the same macrobiotic diet he did. He repeated his offer to give Toby a massage. "Just come to the guest house," he purred, greedily nibbling a raw carrot. "It doesn't matter how late. I have been told, in all modesty, that my fingers are magic."

"So are mine," snorted Cora. "And if you don't stop flirting with this poor girl, my magic fingers will curl around a frying pan and whomp you on the skull."

"Flirting? Really!" sneered the doctor, and extended his invitation again.

"Thanks, but no thanks," Toby said as evenly as she could. Tired as she was, she had to struggle not to snicker at the expression Cora was making behind the doctor's back.

"Moranti!" Jake's voice thundered from the studio. "Are you going to eat all night? We've got work to do!"

"Hark," said Cora, "it's the Viking war cry."

Toby, aching in body and spirit, rose to answer it.

Jake kept her working, reworking, and again reworking the drawings until almost midnight. Toby's mind was muzzy: there was no longer any reality in the world but the room, her drawing hand and Jake's persistent voice. She felt the dogged, instinctive determination to survive of someone on a forced march.

When she completed the finished pencil sketch for the sixth strip, she felt the odd punchiness of a fighter who refused to stay down, no matter how many times he is hit. If Jake wanted to go all night, she would go all night. She didn't know how the adrenaline kept coursing through her fatigued body, yet it did.

Then, mercifully, he told her she could stop. "That's enough," he said gruffly. "You're worn out."

"No, I'm not," she protested, but her words sounded slightly slurred. "I can go on as long as you can."

He gave her a short harsh laugh. "Don't flatter yourself. Go to bed. We can catch up tomorrow."

Pleasant thought, her tired mind said bitterly. But part of her was infinitely grateful that he was letting her go. She pushed back her chair and got up stiffly. Her legs had fallen half asleep, and she stumbled a bit drunkenly against the worktable.

His left arm shot out and caught her around the waist. At his touch, her dulled senses sprang instantly back to life. His arm seemed powerful enough to support her forever, and strength radiated into her body from his lean fingers. He pulled her nearer to him, to help her regain her balance. His piercing blue eyes bore into hers for the skip of a heartbeat. The line of his mouth curved oddly as he looked down at her.

Instinctively she had put her hand on his right shoulder to steady herself. He glanced at it, took a slight step backward and brushed her hand away.

"See?" he said, the line of his lips straight and unreadable again. "You can't even stand up straight."

He said it as if the fact gave him infinite satisfaction. Her heart hammered hard in her chest, and she forced her breathing to slow. "Don't worry," she said, feeling her blood pound with unwarranted swiftness through her body. "I'll do better."

He raised one heavy eyebrow. "That goes without saying. You'll have to. If you want to keep up with me. Good night, Moranti. Sleep tight. And if you dream, try to dream about making those pie-slice eyes right."

He gave her a mocking half smile, turned and left. She bit her lip in anger as she watched his broad back disappear through the door. But in spite of her resentment, there was a catch in her chest at the way his right arm hung almost immobile at his side and at the sight of his black-gloved injured hand.

Conflicting emotions warred with exhaustion in her brain as she mechanically cleaned up. Her whole body hurt, and she was so tense she wondered if she could relax enough to sleep.

After the pens and brushes were back in their resting places, the sheets of paper laid out for tomorrow's work, she stood a moment, rubbing the back of her neck. She looked in weariness down at the stack of strips she had done that day. Idly she flipped through them, examining them panel by panel.

As she did so, her heart began to soar wildly within her. The drawings had cost her more labor, more patience, more spirit than she thought she could give. But there was no question about it. They were the best things she had ever done, better than anything she had dreamed she could do.

The price had been high. She had the frightened feeling Jake would drive it higher still, demanding everything she had. He would possess her, like a demon. He had already begun.

Her body burned when his arm had held her, his hand had touched her, so briefly. Suddenly, in spite of all he had put her through, she wished he had held her longer and that he would hold her again.

Wrong, she thought dizzily. *Wrong, wrong, wrong. Don't have those kinds of feelings. The only parts of you he wants are your hand and your brain. Make the rest of your body and your misguided affections ignore him if you value your sanity.*

She went into the kitchen for a glass of milk. Outside, in the darkness, she heard a horse's nicker and the muffled clatter of hooves. She shuddered slightly. He was out there, she knew, riding that wild-eyed pinto along the treacherous bluffs in the wind and the moonlight.

He's a dangerous man, she warned herself again. *Dangerous and driven.*

CHAPTER FOUR

THE NEXT FIVE DAYS passed in a blur of exhaustion, frustration and the peculiar exhilaration of creation.

For long blocks of time, Toby felt like a galley slave, wrenching herself half dead with work. Jake, unsmiling, intense and impatient, was the unrelenting master who demanded still more from her.

There were moments when he drove her perilously close to tears or an explosion of anger. There were times when she wondered why she had ever deluded herself into thinking that she had an iota of talent or that she could draw at all—times when she'd have gleefully quit, turning her back on him and his impossibly high standards forever. The only thing that kept her going was her icy determination not to be defeated. She was not a quitter, and she had never been.

Yet to her confusion, there were also moments of great satisfaction, even pleasure. She knew she had learned more in this past week than she had in a year of art school. Such moments were so shiveringly intense that she forgot the drudgery and pain they cost. For once in a while she accomplished the impossible. She satisfied Jake. She knew she satisfied him because he would look at her work and give it a curt nod of approval. That was all. It seemed almost enough—until he began his next critical onslaught.

DR. HYDE-CRIPPEN, round, gleaming of pate, and pompous, always hovered in the background, practicing his mysterious ministrations. He did not, however, hover quite far enough back to suit Cora—or Toby. Apparently hoping to start a flirtation with Toby, he began taking his meals with them which meant the two women had little time to talk. Instead, they were forced to listen to Dr. Hyde-Crippen endlessly sing the praises of Dr. Hyde-Crippen.

Jake was becoming increasingly restless and began driving into Zion Bluff to eat supper at his favorite small café. The house was closing in on him, he said. He had to recharge his creative batteries and keep in touch with the heart of small town Americana.

Toby would have liked to recharge *her* own batteries, but instead she found her energy being further drained by having to cope with Hyde-Crippen. And she was sure Cora needed new batteries altogether. The doctor had, according to his own accounts, studied the sciences of medicine—general, preventative and surgical; the arts of chiropractic, massage therapy, traction therapy and electrotherapy. He had learned acupressure in Hong Kong, acupuncture in Taiwan, the secrets of dharana yoga in Bombay, hatha yoga in Rangoon, asana yoga in Pondicherry, and mastered meditation in the mountains of Tibet.

Toby listened to this litany with resignation, Cora with ill-disguised impatience. When the doctor, smug in his own immense self-regard, waddled back to the guest house, Cora rolled her eyes and made such wildly caustic remarks that Toby had to smile.

But behind Cora's barrage of scoffing, Toby sensed worry, ceaseless and deep. Jake was more irritable than ever, and as the week wore on, he seemed in worse pain and under greater stress. Toby and Cora joked uneasily about Hyde-Crippen, but in spite of the man's ridiculously ponderous ego, they both began to fear what harm he could bring to Jake. Of course, Jake would hear nothing against the little man. Cora unhappily held her peace in his presence, but watched Jake carefully. The more the look of pain in his eyes intensified, the harder and more determined the line of his jaw grew. He drove himself without mercy, and he drove Toby as well.

Saturday night the two of them worked well beyond midnight. It was a perfect spring night, surprisingly balmy and drenched with bright moonlight. Cora, exhausted by the emotion of the week, had gone to bed early. The light in Dr. Hyde-Crippen's cottage had long been darkened.

Jake had turned off the studio air conditioner and opened the glass doors to the flagstone patio. The night air was surprisingly mellow, fresh with the gentle scent of summer.

He stood staring out at the river that twinkled far below in the moonlight. He had been forbiddingly quiet all night. Toby breathed the fresh breeze deeply. Outside crickets sang in noisy chorus, and their manic music, combined with the cool fragrance of the air, made her feel both peaceful and light-headed.

She was inking a difficult panel, the last of a Sunday episode. The strip was a particularly outrageous one in which Matilda began her campaign to be elected mayor of Bigalow Springs. The concluding panel depicted Matilda, playing a tuba, leading her supporters in a parade through the main street of town.

It had taken her most of the evening. The perspective was tricky. There were twenty-nine characters in the picture and Toby had learned to her sorrow that drawing a marching kangaroo playing a tuba was a task designed to drive the most patient artist into the far reaches of insanity. In addition, Matilda always wore an Aussie hat with the rim tacked up on one side, and one of the hardest things about drawing her was getting the hat set at precisely the right angle to express Matilda's mood.

She finished inking and sighed with relief. She stared at the panel with a combination of exhaustion and elation. It was the most ambitious and accomplished drawing she'd ever executed.

She was suddenly aware that Jake had moved behind her, looking over her shoulder. A sudden and familiar frisson played up her spine. She wished he would return to his moody vigil staring out at the river. She was too exhausted, too agitated to cope with what his nearness did to her.

"All right," she said almost irritably, trying to ignore the tickling of her nerve endings. "What's wrong with it? Tell me now, while I'm too tired to care."

But he only stood behind her, making the back of her neck feel cold and prickly and her chest swarm with uneasy and unwanted excitement. She refused to turn and look at him. The silence between them made her more and more edgy. Jake must be minutely cataloging the drawing's shortcomings. Only the crickets' wild hymn to the night broke the quiet.

Toby swallowed hard. She still refused to look at him. "Well?" she asked, setting her jaw, waiting for his criticism. "Tell me. What's wrong?"

But again, the only reply was the crickets' song on the river-scented breeze.

"Nothing," he said at last, his voice low, almost grudging. "Nothing's wrong with it, Moranti. It's fine."

She turned slowly in her chair and looked up at him in surprise. She immediately wished she hadn't. The night breeze gently stirred his thick gold hair to a gleaming disorder that made her want to reach up and smooth it. The set of his strong, full mouth was half bitter, half contemplative—almost distant. The haunting azure eyes were not looking at her at all, but past her, at the drawings on the board.

"You're good, Moranti," he said dispassionately. Almost casually, he set his left hand on the nape of her neck. Just as casually, his fingers toyed with the beaded clip Cora had given her, laced themselves in the black wealth of her imprisoned curls. Although the movement was almost a caress, his voice was distant, bored. "Sometimes, you're all right."

"What?" she asked, blinking hard. She wished he would move his hand. She also wished he would not. His touch unsettled her deeply. "Sometimes I'm what?"

He sighed harshly, as if the words weren't worth repeating. "You're all right," he said between clenched teeth. "You may work out. Now get to bed. I've seen enough of you for one day, God knows. You get on my nerves."

He took his hand from her hair and thrust it casually in the back pocket of his faded jeans. He strolled back to the patio doors, then stared out at the bluffs as if she had already left the room.

She looked after him in disbelief, her heart rocking violently. The sight of his rumpled gold hair, his wide shoulders, his narrow hips, loosed a storm of tumult within her.

For a split second, she had rejoiced at his faint praise. But then, his words filled her with bewildered rage. After all he'd put her through, how dare he dismiss her as simply *all right*? How, after all the abuse she'd taken, did he dare say she *might* work out?

How did he dare say he'd seen enough of her for one day, when it was he who set the impossible, nerve-shattering hours she worked? How did he have the effrontery to say she got on *his* nerves? And the gall to order her to bed, as if she were a faithful but slightly dim-witted dog?

She could feel her dark eyes flashing. The back of her neck still tingled where he had touched her. That only fed her anger. What right did he have even to touch her?

"I said, Go to bed, Moranti," he repeated, still staring up at the stars. He rubbed his right bicep, as if the arm bothered him more than usual. In a tone that implied he'd had an afterthought, he added, "Tomorrow's your day off. You can spend it staying out of my way. You and Cora both."

Toby's control over her complex emotions snapped. "Thank you—your majesty," she said vehemently. "Good night—and go to blazes."

At first he didn't bother to turn and face her. He kept his back to her, and remained staring up at the brilliant stars, massaging the muscles of his right arm.

Toby swallowed, her heart beating fast. As soon as she said the words she regretted them. He would probably fire her on the spot. But instead he turned to face her, his left hand still clenched on his aching right arm. He was pale beneath his tan, and for the first time Toby realized how much pain he was in.

"You mean, 'Go to hell'?" he asked, with his maddening half-crooked smile. "Too late, Moranti. I've already been there, and I'm on my way back. No matter what anybody thinks."

Her eyes locked with his for an uncomfortable split second. Shame flooded through her. She dropped her gaze from his. "I'm sorry," she said, her anger and her energy both shriveled to nothingness. "I—you—we're both under pressure. I forget what you're going through—I didn't mean it." She rose to go. She wanted only to escape.

Her apology seemed to galvanize him in a way her anger could not. His eyes shot fire at her. In an instant, he was at her side, towering above her, his head bent over hers. He gripped her right wrist with his good hand, and Toby's face turned up in alarm to stare at him.

"I don't ever want to hear that again," he said, his voice filled with threat. His eyes narrowed under the thick bronze brows and a muscle jerked in his jaw. "And I don't ever want to see that again."

"Hear what?" she asked, trying to step back in confusion. "See what?" But his hand was too strong and she could neither break his grip nor move away from him.

"That you're sorry," he commanded, his voice taut. "You know what drives me craziest about you, Moranti? I never wanted you here at all, but what really makes me crazy is the damned pity I see in your eyes. I'd rather have you tell me to go to hell every hour of the day than see that pity. Because I don't need it. I don't want it. And I won't have it."

Shaken and frightened by the passion in his voice, she spoke without thinking. "I'm sorry," she said again, then bit her lip as he gripped her wrist harder and shook her.

"And I said," he ordered, teeth clenched, bending closer to her, "don't ever say that to me. Ever. I'm not down. I'm not out. I'm not through. I know neither you nor Cora believe that, but I don't give a damn what you think. You stay here as long as I can use you. Which won't be long."

"I'm not sorry for you," Toby countered, tears of perplexity and pain springing to her eyes. "I'm just sorry this job ever came up, and I'm sorry I took it. Who could be sorry for you? You're too nasty to pity!"

But even as she spoke, she knew she was lying, for her feelings for Jake had been mixed with pity—large amounts of it—from the start, and she suddenly realized he was far too strong a man to ever accept it.

"Oh," he said with a low and bitter laugh. "Sorry you're here? Do you want to turn tail and go home? Just when you're starting to learn something? Go ahead—leave. I wouldn't miss you."

"You'd love that, wouldn't you?" she said, her anger returning and her own voice dangerously edged. "You'd love to chase me off. Well, you can't. You'd like to think you're so ferocious you could run me off like a mouse. Well, think again, Ulrick. Whatever you can dish out, I can take."

She tried to twist away from him, but still he held her fast. His mouth kept the bitter smile that never reached his eyes. "Can you?" he demanded, drawing her a step closer in spite of her resistance. "Good. Because dish it out I will. I told you from the beginning—if you work for me, I own you— body and soul."

Toby stared up at him defiantly, her heart beating crazily in her chest. The first time he had made that claim, she ignored it. This time she could not. "Nobody owns me. *Nobody*—"

His jaw tightened. A frown line sprang to angry life between his brows. "Yes," he contradicted. "I do."

"Hardly," she shot back, raising her chin higher.

He brought his face closer to hers, his upper lip curling. "Yes. Completely."

She thrust one hand against his chest in an ineffectual attempt to push him away. She couldn't budge him, but her fingers stayed tensed against him, and she could feel the heat of his body contrasting with the coolness of the night air, which had filled the room.

"You've rented my services, that's all," she said, angrily, but she was starting to feel dizzy. She and Jake were arguing with ruthless ardor, yet she felt something even more powerful surging between them, and it frightened her.

"No." He laughed condescendingly, pulling her closer still. A bare six inches separated them. She felt the hard beat of his heart beneath her fingers and could smell the faint scent of soap and hay that emanated from him. "Not rented. Owned outright. For the duration. When we work, you think the way I tell you to think. You act the way I tell you to act. And by God, you draw the way I tell you to draw. You don't question, and you don't complain. You just do it. My way."

Toby gasped because she both wanted and didn't want his electrifying nearness; it filled her with fear and desire. "You," she whispered desperately, "are the most despicable, overbearing, difficult—"

But with a movement that seemed effortless, he pulled her more closely still, until she could feel the pressure of his chest against her breast, his leg burning against hers. "Quiet, Moranti," he commanded. His blue eyes looked almost languid, yet somehow still maintained their para-doxical intensity. "I'm about to show you who's boss."

No! she thought wildly. He was going to kiss her. She had known it from the moment he had touched her earlier. Worse, she had wanted him to, as much as she had ever wanted anything in her life.

He lowered his face the few inches that remained between them, and his mouth took hers with such undeniable absolute confidence that she would not and could not resist him. His lips were sure yet questing against her own, claiming and searching at the same time. Without wanting to, she found herself rising on tiptoe to make his touch more intimate, more rousing.

When she made that slight and involuntary movement toward him, he released her wrist and cupped her chin, as if her kiss were something he would drink until he was totally satiated. Somehow, his right arm was around her body, and although the lower part of it was immobile, the strong muscles of the upper half pinioned her more firmly against the virile length of his body. She felt his long and muscled thighs, the hardness of his chest. She shuddered with unwanted rapture at the exploring heat of his lips, the gentle but inexorable pressure of his fingers, tracing first the satiny line of her jaw, then moving to caress the feathery thickness of her lashes, the winglike curve of her eyebrow.

The hand she had pressed in protest against his chest rose, without her volition, and slipped to his neck, feeling its strength and the pounding of his pulse. Her other hand lifted almost fearfully to touch the warmth of his straining shoulder muscles.

At that second shy but unmistakable response from her, Jake's kiss quickened into a flame that no longer merely warmed, but ravished. He seemed determined to obliterate all the world except the hunger for touch. Although the sensations he created in her were wildly pleasurable, there was something nearly savage in him that frightened her,

both for the power it revealed in him and the need it un-
veiled within herself.

Toby's mind threatened to collapse into pure sensual sur-
render as his body molded itself more demandingly against
hers and his lips stole away her will. Yet Jake's ardor terri-
fied her almost as much as it enticed her, and she felt herself recoiling from him in sheer self-preservation. He had
touched her, kissed her, taken her to him as no other man
had ever done, and yet, despite the tumult he stirred in her,
she recognized what he was doing: he was drawing her
inexorably under his power, subduing her mind and spirit to
his own.

"No!" she protested brokenly, dragging her lips away
from his. Her arms dropped from his neck, his shoulder,
and she tried to extricate herself from his fevering embrace.
"No," she said again, almost sobbing.

"Why not?" he asked, his breath hot against her ear.
"You wanted me to kiss you, didn't you?"

She drew away swiftly and awkwardly, but he did not try
to stop her. She no longer knew what she wanted. But she
knew what she did not want. She did not want that feeling
of helplessness before the primal power of his sexuality. She
stared up at him, trying to gather her forces to make a magic
circle to ward him off.

"No," she said raggedly, rubbing her fingertips across her
swollen lips. "I didn't."

He shrugged, smiling slightly. "Yes. You did. Only not
that way. You wanted the wilted kiss of some suffering sop
of an invalid—some poetic type who needs your strength.
Well, that's not me. Get that through your head."

She could only stare at him defensively, as she might at a
dangerous predator. He reached toward her. She flinched,
but he only chucked her under the chin flippantly. "I told
you, Moranti," he said coolly. "I'm in charge. Consider me
the lord and master around here—for as long as I let you
stay."

I will not, she wanted to scream. But she could say nothing. She could only watch him in angry wariness.

He turned casually. "If you're not going to bed, I will," he said, stifling a yawn. "Since you don't want to turn in, you can clean the brushes and pens. Good night."

He strolled into the hallway, rubbing his upper arm absently, and Toby stared after him. Her body trembled, shaken and exhausted. Her mind felt as if it hovered at the edge of pure darkness and chaos.

Mechanically she cleaned the drawing implements. Mechanically she went to her room and climbed into bed. But there was nothing mechanical in the way she cried into her pillow.

How stupid she had been to deny he owned her. She had adored him since she was sixteen years old and had been dazzled for the first time by the powerful brilliance of "Heartland." She had idolized him and belonged to him long before they ever met.

Her dilemma was that she loved the artist but feared the man. But did the artist even exist any longer? Was an artist who could no longer draw still an artist? What kind of man had he been, and what kind was he becoming? If she didn't pity him, she had to beware of him. Yet, paradoxically, some heedless part of her desired him. She could see no way for all this complexity to end, except badly.

In spite of her brave words that he could not force her to leave, she suddenly wanted to flee for her life. She was nothing except a tool Jake was forced to use. That was all. He would never condescend to treat her as a human being. He could only be satisfied by dominating her totally. He resented having to depend on her. He would compensate by trying to master and crush her will as completely as he could. Then she, not he, would be the dependent one.

Something within her almost accepted that domination, and it frightened her as nothing ever had. The situation was more complicated and painful than she could have imagined. On some deep and primitive level, she found him too compelling. She had to leave here. She had to. Monday she would give him her two weeks' notice.

"SOMETHING HAPPENED; don't tell me it didn't," Cora accused, wheeling the Cadillac around a particularly frightening curve. "Last night. After I went to bed. Don't deny it. I could feel it coming. The way a person feels a thunderstorm coming."

"Nothing happened," Toby lied unhappily. She stared moodily out the window at the sun-drenched landscape. She hadn't found the nerve yet to tell Cora of her decision to leave.

"Ha," challenged Cora. She had let Toby sleep late, forced her to eat a huge country breakfast, then practically kidnapped her, insisting the younger woman needed to get out of the house for a change and do something besides bend over a drawing board.

"Ha, yourself," Toby said morosely, still staring at the wooded hills and green pastures. She had spent the morning delivering sermons to herself; she had to stop remembering the touch and taste of Jake's lips. What had happened between them the night before was senseless and best forgotten. It would not happen again. She would leave. She would forget it.

"Where are we going, anyway?" Toby asked, turning to look at Cora. She had no right to inflict her bad mood on the other woman.

Cora was spiffed out in her Sunday best—a pale blue satin shirt, white slacks and white calfskin pumps. Her black hair was pulled back in a gleaming chignon, and silver bangles swung from her ears. She wore a bracelet with the biggest turquoise Toby had ever seen, and her fingers were covered with silver rings. Toby, in muted green terry shorts and halter, felt distinctly dowdy beside her.

"It's a secret," Cora said impassively. "A surprise."

Toby groaned. "I can't stand any more secrets. This place has made me crazy with secrets. Tell me where we're going— please."

"Nope," Cora replied, giving her a rueful smile. "I told you. It's a surprise. Try me on another subject."

Cora, as usual, had classical music blasting from the tape deck. Firmly Toby reached over and turned the music down. "All right," she said, challenging. She might be leaving, but she wanted some answers before she did. "I'll try you on a couple of other subjects. And if you don't finally give me some information—"

"You'll do what, paleface?" laughed Cora. "Steal my land?"

Toby grinned in spite of herself. She was going to miss this down-to-earth irreverent woman, even if she had known her only a short time.

"Just tell me, Cora. Why all the secrets around here? Who's Denise? What happened to Raynor? And Jake's parents? Why all the hush-hush?"

"Well," Cora said, tilting her head and shrugging, "you should be able to figure out why all the secrets. Jake's a private person. Very private."

"Doesn't he take it a little far?" Toby objected. "I mean, cartoonists aren't like film stars or royalty or something— gossip magazines don't care about them. Reporters don't camp on their doorsteps."

"We've had a few reporters try," Cora returned. "Jake's not just any cartoonist. He happens to be the best one alive. His work belongs to the public. But he's private."

"But he's too private," Toby protested. "That's the problem. Why such a passion for privacy?"

"He's also proud," Cora said evenly. "In case you haven't noticed."

Toby sank more deeply into the plush blue seat of the Cadillac and sighed. "I've noticed, all right. He's proud. He certainly doesn't want anybody's pity—he's made that clear."

"Ah," Cora said, nodding. "You clashed over that. I should have guessed. Toby, he lived to draw. Now he can't. He's forced to let you do it for him. Look, it's natural he resents that. And nothing ever made him more furious than somebody feeling sorry for him. Don't take it personally, okay?"

Toby shook her head, biting her lip. "I understand that," she managed to say. "I've tried not to take it personally, but..."

"But he's too hard on you, right?" Cora asked, tapping her ringed fingers against the steering wheel impatiently. "Try to understand. He doesn't want to need anybody for anything. Ever. Now he needs you. He has to learn he's going to keep right on needing you—or somebody. He's doesn't know how to need anybody—yet."

Toby glanced out the window at the lush fields once again. Cora's words hurt, although they shouldn't. Jake needed only her drawing hand—the loan of a trained hand.

Cora cast her a brief speculative look, trying to read the strange expression on Toby's face. "There are reasons he's this way," Cora said at last. "Oh, believe me, he'll do his best to drive you off, but, for his sake, I don't want you to go. And I know you're thinking of leaving—aren't you?"

Toby continued to look out the window. She didn't want to meet Cora's eyes. She nodded hopelessly. "I'm leaving as soon as I can," she admitted at last. "And, frankly, I don't know why you're so loyal to him. He may be a genius, but he's also a beast."

There was a moment of silence. "He's a man," Cora replied finally. "And the closest thing to a son I've got. I've loved him for twenty-four years, sunshine and shadow. Right now, it's mostly shadow."

Almost against her will, Toby turned her eyes toward Cora. The older woman's face was solemn as she stared at the highway. In spite of her Sunday finery, she suddenly looked tired and almost old.

"Ever see a reservation?" she asked, not waiting for an answer, the line of her mouth grim. "A government reservation? I grew up on one. And vowed I'd never stay. So like a fool, I married to escape. That didn't work, so I went to work for old Reverend and Mrs. Ulrick—Jake's grandparents. A hired girl was all I had the education to be. I wanted better, but it looked like I'd never have a chance to get it. For a long time, it seemed like life didn't have much point or meaning. Then along came the boys—*my* boys."

"Jake," Toby breathed, watching Cora's somber face. "And—the other one? Raynor?"

"Jacob and Raynor," Cora nodded. "Jake and Rayn. Identical twins. They ended up with their grandparents because their mother died in childbirth, and their father—well, he never did give a damn for anyone except himself—a handsome devil he was. A major in the air force. Couldn't keep dragging those boys all over the face of the earth, he said, so he dumped them in that cheerless old house with those cheerless old people. Oh, he'd take the boys back from time to time, but he always dumped them again because they interfered with his women, and he did like the women. Married six of them before he was through."

Toby's dark eyes widened. "Six?" she asked in disbelief. She came from a tight-knit family where marriages lasted a lifetime. Six marriages seemed as excessive as six heads.

Cora nodded curtly. "Those boys had so many step-mothers, they couldn't keep them straight. About the time they'd get used to one, there'd be a new one. Sometimes the women would talk the major into taking the boys back, but it never lasted. Home they'd come, if anybody could call the reverend's house a home.

"Their grandfather, the reverend, died when they were fourteen. The old woman, Mrs. Ulrick, she just kind of gave up. Retreated inside herself. On her bad days, she couldn't even remember who the boys were or how she got them. But somehow they survived—because they had each other, I suppose—and the paper world."

"The paper world?" Toby asked, her throat constricted.

"Kids are marvelous creatures," Cora said with admiration. "Resilient. Jake and Rayn did what thousands of other children do—they escaped from a not-very-pleasant reality into a make-believe world—a world they created. When they started drawing, they called it 'paper world.' It was a lot like Zion Bluff, only better—and funny—and all the things that could cause pain became merely laughable. They were the rulers. And you know what it became, don't you?"

"Heartland," Toby answered softly. "They created 'Heartland'—when they were just kids."

"Right," Cora said brusquely. "They knew from the start what they wanted to do when they grew up—work together on the 'funnies' and be one of the great teams. You never saw boys so centered on one goal. After the reverend died, they filled their room with funnies—comics everywhere! They studied them. They devoured them. They must have dreamed them."

"And you," questioned Toby, looking at Cora with new respect, "just what were you doing through all this? Holding everything together, I'll bet. Admit it, Cora—you were the only stable person in their lives—the one that gave them any security they had."

Cora looked embarrassed. "We got along. I mean, of course, I tried to make them happy—somebody had to. And although old woman Ulrick looked down on their drawing, I knew they should be encouraged. I knew they were special. And somehow the three of us were on the same wavelength. Especially Jake and I. Oh, Lordy, the fights we had. He's like me—won't back down for the devil himself. Raynor was the charmer. The lighthearted one and the gentle one, and I loved him, but Jake, for all his faults, was the one

I understood best. Maybe because he hasn't got one atom of the quitter in him."

"And Raynor?" Toby asked, her voice tentative. "What happened to Raynor?"

"Raynor died," Cora said bluntly. "He drowned. They were twenty years old that summer—getting ready for their junior year at the university. That was the year they were going to start publishing 'Heartland' in the campus paper. They were rafting on the Missouri with friends. Raynor decided to cool off with a swim and dived in. He must have hit something. He didn't come up. Jake went down after him again and again, till he was exhausted and the others had to restrain him. He was like a crazy man. They didn't find the body till that night. It almost killed Jake. Me, too."

She was silent a long moment. "I can't tell you what it was like around here. Old Mrs. Ulrick never understood. She'd look at Jake and say, 'Aren't there supposed to be two of you? Where's the other one? What have you done with him?' But she wasn't the worst. The worst was Denise."

"Denise?" Toby asked carefully. Denise was the woman with the long loose hair, and it was her memory Jake wanted to avoid.

"A beautiful girl," Cora said grudgingly. "But awfully self-centered. They met her at the university and I think both boys were in love with her. But she chose Raynor. Like I said, he was the charmer, the easygoing one. They were engaged."

Cora sighed deeply. "Her family lived in Omaha. Jake refused to phone her when Raynor died. He'd been up most of the night helping look for the body, and when they found it, he insisted on driving down to tell her in person. He got there at five in the morning, and he just sat in the car until nine, waiting for the household to wake up. He wanted her to be able to face it on a good night's sleep. And when he told her, she collapsed in his arms. For the next three days she couldn't even talk, and all she could do was hang on to

Jake. She made it through the funeral only because he held her up. She made it through the next year only because he kept holding her up.''

She cast Toby a cynical look. ''You can guess what happened. They were both in shock from Rayn's death. They found consolation in each other. Then, in their senior year, it was Jake and Denise who were engaged. Then something—I never knew quite what—happened. It seemed as if she woke up out of a long daze. She told Jake she didn't want the insecurity of being married to an artist. Maybe it was an excuse. After all, Raynor was an artist, too. Maybe she realized she didn't love him, only Raynor's memory. Maybe she realized she never loved either of them. All I know is she gave the ring back. Six weeks later she married some fancy doctor and moved to Baltimore. It did something to Jake—something he never got over. He sort of closed up more than ever—except to a small circle of people. People in Zion Bluff mostly. And he survived the way he always did—by working—working in the paper world.''

Toby contemplated the story and bit her lower lip. No wonder Jake insisted on privacy. He was far too proud a man to let the outside world glimpse the lonely childhood he and Raynor had endured, with only Cora and their own fertile imaginations for protection. Nor did he care for the world to know anything else he had suffered.

''There were some lean times at first,'' Cora went on, weariness evident in her voice. ''He came home, worked at what he could, kept working on the strip. Took care of his grandmother till she died. About that time, the Lincoln paper picked up 'Heartland,' then Omaha did, Grand Island, Des Moines—the rest is history. Though he'll always think of that strip as half Raynor's.''

''I see,'' Toby said, although she was only beginning to. She wondered sadly how Jake could be anything except bitter. His history was a heritage of loss.

"He's tough," Cora said grimly. "He's survived it all—his mother's death, his crazy father, all those stepmothers, grandparents who were as cold as icicles—losing Raynor, and then Denise and now the use of his hand. I don't think he ever felt sorry for himself a moment in his life. He was too intense, and he knew too well what he wanted to do."

Cora paused a moment. "When Denise went, I think she took most of his faith in human nature with her. Although to this day he won't speak against her."

Toby sighed. "All right, Cora. You've convinced me. He's made of stern stuff. And it's no wonder he's ready to lash out at the world, but—"

"No buts," Cora said brusquely. "He could face anything as long as he could draw, create. But now he can't—not without help. I don't know how long he can delude himself with Hyde-Crippen, but sooner or later he's got to admit he isn't going to draw again. He needs you, whether he likes it or not. And I've seen your stuff, Toby. He's not going to find anybody better than you. I doubt if he'll find anybody half as good."

"Cora," Toby said tiredly, "I'd like to be able to tell you that flattery will get you everywhere, but—"

"I'm not flattering you," Cora corrected. "I'm telling the truth. I'll also tell you Jake will put you through holy hell—if you let him. I know how his mind works. The syndicate forced you on him, so he'll retaliate by trying to show you he doesn't need you—and keeping you in your place any way he can. When he gets that way, you just fight him back, that's all. I didn't survive all these years with him by keeping my mouth shut, I guarantee you."

That's fine, Toby thought grimly. Usually she could stand up for her rights as well as anybody and better than most. But when Jake's domination entered the realm of the physical and emotional, she felt inexperienced, vulnerable—and frightened. She did not want to admit this to Cora. The memory of the night before scalded too much.

But the older woman seemed to read her mind. "A lot of women have wanted him, you know," Cora said carefully. "Not that it's done them any good—especially since that damned Denise. Let's face it—Jake doesn't have the rosiest view of women. To him they're like his horses, strictly for recreation. He loves his work. He loves Zion Bluff—in his way. But I'm not sure he's capable of loving anything else. It's—well—dangerous for an outsider to care for him. I owe you that much. To tell you. Since Denise, he's hurt a lot of women—without even trying."

"If you're warning me not to get emotionally involved with him," Toby said carefully, "I've already figured that out."

"Try—" Cora said, and her tone was suddenly close to pleading "—try to keep some emotional distance from him. Stand up to him when he needs standing up to, ignore him when you have to, and you'll be fine—really."

"Cora," Toby began, her mind disintegrating into confusion again, "I just don't think I can—"

Almost without her noticing it, they had entered a small city with a sign at the limits that read Norfolk. Cora was wheeling the Cadillac into a lot full of shiny cars with big numbers crayoned on the windshields. Colored pennants fluttered overhead lazily in the breeze.

"What are we doing?" Toby asked. "Does your car need work? Is this place even open?"

"It's sort of open—just for you," Cora said, halting the Cadillac with a slight screech. "Old man Munson should be along any minute. We're a little early. I guess I was speeding again."

"What do you mean—open just for me?" Toby asked in perplexity.

"When Jake hired you, he specified you provide your own transportation. Well, he hasn't given you time to even look for anything. He knows you've worked harder than he had any right to ask. So he's leased something for you. He'll pick up the bill. I think it's that one over there."

She nodded at a sleek classic sixties Mustang—one of the great cars of that decade—a collector's prize. Perfectly restored, it gleamed in the bright noon sunshine. It was a flamboyant shade of azure blue that Cora told her had been created especially for Nebraska's centennial.

Toby's lips parted in wonder. It was the most marvelous car she'd ever seen: the kind of car she'd always dreamed of. But she felt a sinking sensation as well.

"I can't let him do that. It's too much. When did he decide to do this?" Surely, she thought, it had to be prior to the night before, when things had exploded between them.

Cora shrugged, refusing to look at her. "This morning. I know something happened last night, Toby. Whatever it was, he regrets it. Jake's not the type to apologize. This is his way of making a peace offering."

Toby looked at the lovely azure curves of the Mustang, but shook her head in negation. "It's beautiful, Cora. But he can't buy me. That's that."

Cora faced her, putting her hand on Toby's. Her black eyes were intent. "It means more than that, Toby. This means he wants you to stay...do you *know* how important that is?"

She felt tears rising. "Maybe it does mean he wants me to stay—and maybe that's a good sign—but I can't. And I told you, he can't buy me. I'm not for sale."

"Toby," Cora said, gripping the younger woman's hand more tightly. "Stay. Don't stay because of the car. Stay because of him. Stay for him, for his sake. And for mine."

Cora's voice was shaking, and she was close to begging. Toby's heart wrenched within her, for she knew how hard it must be for Cora to beg for anything.

"Please," Cora said intensely. "Stay. So he can continue to create. He may never draw again, but 'Heartland's' still inside him, in his imagination. And you can put it on paper, make it live.''

Toby's thoughts cascaded in uncontrollable tumult. Jake was apologizing, in his brusque and high-handed way. He wanted her to stay. But what more did he want? Perhaps to show her he could own her body and soul—for as long as he chose. It was all madness.

"You'll stay, won't you?" Cora asked, the same tremor in her voice, the same desperate determination in her eyes.

And Toby, who could not be bought, also knew that she was helpless to deny a plea from a woman whose emotions were as honest as Cora's.

"I'll stay," she said at last. She stared out the window at the blue Mustang, but she didn't really see it. Instead, in her mind's eye, she saw Jake's face, handsome, bitter, taunting, and stony with the stubbornness of the undefeatable.

"Good girl," Cora said, patting her hand fondly. "From the first time I saw you, I knew you had what it takes."

Toby gave Cora's hand a squeeze in return, but she wondered, deep within her, if she had what it took at all—or if she had just made the worst decision of her life.

CHAPTER FIVE

As MUCH AS SHE WANTED to resist it, Toby fell in love with the Mustang almost immediately. She was to follow Cora back to Zion Bluff, but Cora, full of impatient energy as usual, soon left her behind in a cloud of dust.

Toby switched the radio on, found a station playing upbeat, cheery music, and settled into savoring the performance of the car.

"All right, Baby Blue," she murmured to the Mustang. "You're the best bribe I've ever got in my life. In fact you're the only bribe I've ever got in my life. But I'm considering you a bonus—well earned—for putting up with Jake Ulrick for a full week. Come to think of it, he's so impossible, you should be a Rolls-Royce. Or possibly a Lear Jet."

She tried to feel cynical about the car, but Jake's gesture touched and disturbed her more than she cared to admit. What, she wondered, just what if he really did want her to stay—and not just because he needed her to draw his strip? What if his kisses the previous night had been more than a simple release of the anger and tension simmering between them? What if they had meant more?

She frowned, tried to push the thought aside. *Impossible,* she said to herself. That would mean he cared for her, even slightly, and Cora had spelled out the unlikelihood of that. "A lot of women have wanted him. Not that it's done them any good... Women are like his horses—strictly for recreation.... It's dangerous to care for him.... Keep some distance...."

Yes, Cora had laid it on the line, and clearly, too.

So what did the temporary gift of the Mustang mean? Was it a peace offering, as Cora suggested, or was more at stake? By accepting the car, by agreeing to staying, was she compromising herself? Did he think by impressing her with his power and money, he could wipe from her memory any resentment—make her forget the way he treated her? Would that mean another replay of the scene the night before?

She winced at the thought. For the truth was that in spite of Jake's mystery and arrogance, he exercised an enticing attraction for her—one she must resist if she was to maintain any integrity at all.

Or—her mind started to churn painfully—did it mean he was finally on the brink of admitting that the silly doctor, Hyde-Crippen, could do nothing for him, and he would have to accept an assistant? And would that cause him to appreciate her—or to hate her?

At this point, her head begin to ache. She wished she were not driving through the bright Nebraska sunlight in this marvelous car. She wished she was not living in a great house overlooking the Missouri River and working for the most brilliant man in her field. She wished devoutly that she were back in North Bergen, in her cramped apartment next to the laundromat. She wished she had nothing to drive but the rusting clunker she had bought from her brother Dean. And she wished she still worked, unchallenged and harmlessly bored, on the dull adventures of the kindly, predictable old Dr. Dinsmore.

TOBY, PERTURBED and excited, wasn't paying sufficient attention to detail when she got back to the house and parked the car and got out. Troubled, she gazed out at the wide brown river, thinking of all that Cora had told her. She should have been looking at the ground beneath her feet instead. She took a misstep on the flagstone walk behind the house and turned her ankle.

"Damn!" she muttered with feeling. She sat down hard on a garden bench and rubbed her ankle. It stung miserably, and she felt clumsy and foolish, glad nobody had seen her stumble. This would teach her to lose herself in fruitless thought.

"May I be of service?" asked an ingratiating voice near her ear.

Toby gave a start. Dr. Hyde-Crippen stood right behind her, looking more bizarre than usual. Shirtless, he wore a baggy pair of plaid bathing trunks that came nearly to his hairy little knees. The skin of his shoulders, sunken chest and protruding belly were mottled by the start of a sunburn. He smelled of cocoa butter and had so much zinc oxide on his nose it resembled a white beak. He peered at her over the tops of a pair of cheap sunglasses, and he held an orange silk umbrella over his balding head.

"I said, 'May I be of service?'" the small man repeated, a bit too eagerly. "I've been taking a bit of the sun—with the appropriate protective measures, of course," he added.

Toby, still rubbing her ankle, glanced beyond him to the patio. He had obviously been stretched out in a lounge chair. On the wrought iron table beside the lounger was a small portable fan and a drink that looked suspiciously like a vodka tonic—except, of course, Hyde-Crippen loathed the very thought of alcohol.

"My pride's hurt more than anything," she replied ruefully. "The greatest service you could do is forget the sight of me tripping."

"Tush and nonsense," tutted Hyde-Crippen. "You're in pain. And I, if you will recall, am a healer. Take the lounge chair. I don't think you're hurt badly. And I can give you relief."

Before Toby could protest, he had her by the arm and was steering her toward the lounge chair, where she reclined, half embarrassed and against her will. It looked as if Hyde-Crippen was going to get his magic fingers on her at last, and there was nothing she could do, short of being rude, to avoid it.

The doctor's pudgy hands fluttered over her ankle with surprising lightness. His touch was as delicate as that of a moth. "Ah," he said with obvious pleasure, "not serious at all—a mere strain, not even a sprain. I'll give you relief in no time."

Before Toby could object, he was behind her. Then, to her amazement, his fingers moved to the back of her neck. "This hurts, doesn't it?" He stated rather than asked, and Toby was surprised that her neck did indeed hurt in that spot. Pressing the painful region, Hyde-Crippen moved his other hand to Toby's forehead. "And it hurts you here," he said with triumph. Again amazed, Toby realized that the spot he touched was tender, although she hadn't noticed it before.

"Tum-te-tum-te-tum," hummed the little man. He kept his fingers on the pressure points. "This will fix you up."

"How can you fix my foot by pressing on my neck and my forehead?" Toby asked suspiciously. She couldn't see him because he stood behind her, but she could smell the reek of his cocoa butter.

"Tum-te-tum-te-tum," he caroled. "Where do you think the nerve impulses from that ankle go, my luscious dear? Right up to your pretty spine and into your lovely head."

Well, Toby thought wryly, it made a sort of peculiar sense. Oddly, the little man's touch made the tension in her mind and body relax a bit. The plump fingers fluttered to another point at the back of her neck, another spot on her forehead.

"My, but aren't we full of tension this afternoon?" he said heartily. "You could do with this more often, my dear. Your muscles are stiff as starch. You need therapeutic massage on a regular basis. If you'd care to come to my cottage of an evening..."

"Please," Toby said firmly. "Just fix my foot, will you? I'm not the kind of woman who goes in for massages. Therapeutic or otherwise."

"Ah," he sighed. "What a closed mind lies behind that pretty face." His fingers fluttered to two new pressure points, and Toby, against her will, had to admit the little man's touch was making her feel distinctly odd, almost languid.

"You will consent to a massage of your ankle," he asserted at last. "We want to stimulate the blood flow back to your heart. Oh, the body is such a marvelous machine. I love it so."

Before Toby knew what was happening, Hyde-Crippen was at the other end of the lounge, her ankle held gently in his hands. He had stripped off her sandal, and was sensuously massaging her ankle. "I do love a narrow, high-arched foot," he purred. Without warning, he lifted her foot and kissed her on the instep, then continued his massage.

Toby looked at him in disbelief—this peculiar gnome of a man had colossal nerve. She wondered if he really had been drinking.

"I'm trying to make this as nice for you as I can." He smirked over the top of his sunglasses. The sun gleamed on his bald head, which was also turning a mottled pink.

"I'm sure you are," Toby answered, trying to keep the sarcasm out of her voice.

"How cozy," said a heart-shakingly familiar voice. Stunned, Toby looked up to see Jake at the foot of the walk. He wore black swimming trunks and an unbuttoned short-sleeved white shirt. There was water spray in his sun-streaked and tousled hair, and his cheekbones shone like bronze. He played absently with a set of keys in his left hand. He had obviously been out boating on the river, which would give Cora fits. He eyed Toby and Hyde-Crippen with sardonic disdain.

"Excuse me," Jake said sarcastically. "I didn't realize my guests were getting along quite this well. Didn't mean to interrupt. Cheers."

He favored them with a tight, knowing smile and strode with casual feline grace past them, across the patio and into the house.

Toby sighed with frustration. She prayed he hadn't seen Hyde-Crippen plant that ridiculous kiss on her foot, but she knew he had. "I think I've had about enough of this, Doctor," she said severely, extricating her foot from his stroking grasp. She snatched her sandal up and put it on, gritting her teeth as the straps crossed her sore ankle.

"He can be a vile man to work for," Hyde-Crippen said conspiratorially. "Temper of a rabid wolf. It's no wonder you're tense. I know what he's putting you through, my dear, and I speak on your behalf all the time. But be sure that you have a loyal and admiring friend in me, and as I say, any evening you should decide to come to my cottage, I would be glad to pleasure you with such comforts as I can."

"Thank you," Toby said in a choked voice. "But I think not." She rose and hobbled away as quickly as she could. She didn't look back at the maddening little troll. Cora was right. The man was an unscrupulous quack. Her ankle hurt just as badly as before—or almost—and now Jake probably thought she was trying to seduce his personal physician.

Up in the luxury of her tower room, she stared down at the patio. Hyde-Crippen was back in his lounge chair, his portable fan trained on his oiled belly, his umbrella held above his sun-sensitive head. Quack, she thought again bitterly. She was sure he had been drinking. Hypocrite, she thought. How could a man like Jake be taken in by such a smarmy charlatan?

She reclined on her bed, put a hot compress on her ankle and began to try to work on her own star-crossed strip,

"Taffy." She hardly noticed, an hour later, that the pain in her ankle had faded almost completely. And when Cora called her down for supper, she waltzed down the stairs as if she had never hurt herself at all.

She forgot the pain had ever existed until she entered the kitchen and saw Hyde-Crippen sitting at the table. He was blotched with sunburn, and he still smelled of cocoa butter and perspiration, but he looked at her with smug triumph in his little eyes.

"Your ankle is fine now, isn't it, my dear?" he said, beaming. Then he gave her a wink that bordered on the lewd.

No, she thought in stubborn disbelief. He hadn't helped her. She simply hadn't been hurt that bad, that was all. He was tricky, that's all. Clever and very, very tricky.

Throughout supper, he smirked at her more than usual, to her discomfort and Cora's disgust.

After supper, Hyde-Crippen mercifully disappeared to his cottage, and Toby helped Cora load the dishwasher.

"That little phony," Cora fairly snarled, nodding in the direction of the guest house. "I went into the cottage today to clean. I took a good look around and walked right back out. I'm not cleaning up after that two-faced little swine."

"Why?" Toby asked apprehensively. "What did you find?"

"The front part of the cottage is fine—dusty but fine," Cora grumbled. "That's where he has all his weird equipment and torture machines and his typewriter. But his bedroom—yech! The man is disgusting. Phony as a three-dollar bill. Over there he eats his brown rice and talks about purifying the body. But in his room, he's smoking cigars, hitting a bottle of cheap vodka, and under his bed—like a sneaky little child would do—he's hidden a pile of greasy hamburger wrappers and French-fry cartons. Not to mention some girlie magazines that could bring instant death on him in certain feminist circles."

Toby and Cora exchanged a baleful glance. So Hyde-Crippen's hypocrisy extended not merely to vodka, but furtive cigars, secret junk-food orgies and nasty magazines. Somehow it figured, she thought wearily, wondering again why Jake didn't see through the odious man.

"Are you going to tell Jake?" she asked at last.

"No," Cora said glumly. "He thinks I'm prejudiced. He's right—I am, dammit. Jake's the type who always has to find things out for himself. Stubborn devil. But he can't go on trusting that idiot much longer."

Toby shifted uncomfortably, testing her ankle. Hypocrite the man might be, and idiot he might seem, but what if he had actually healed her ankle? What if there were more to him than either she or Cora wanted to admit? For Jake's sake, she suddenly wished there were.

Impossible, she assured herself. The man was ridiculous, an impostor and poseur.

When they finished the dishes, Cora had a phone call from someone named Herbert, so Toby left her in privacy and went to the tower room. Again she tried to make some innovations on her drawings for "Taffy," but nothing worked. She shook her head in frustration. She thought she had learned so much this past week. Why couldn't she carry the knowledge over into her own work? For an irrational moment she resented Jake, as if he were some sort of talent vampire, who took the best of her for his own use.

Now that, she warned herself sternly, *is really wallowing in self-pity and playing destructive mind games.* If she couldn't improve "Taffy," it was her own fault, nobody else's. Besides, she thought, despite a day of rest, she still felt close to emotional exhaustion. How could she concentrate on her personal work?

The next day, she thought with exasperation, she would be immersed in Jake's work again—all day long, for six interminable days. Suddenly the spacious tower room seemed confining, claustrophobic, an air-conditioned and silken prison.

She tried to amuse herself by doing caricatures of Jake—wrote captions under them: "The Artist Contemplating the Wonder of Himself," "The Artist in a Bad Mood" and the funniest, "The Artist and His Ego." She represented the Ego as an enormous, stupid-looking pet monster on a leash. The artist stroked it fondly, and the Ego, fangs grinning, simpered in satisfaction.

The drawings had a nervous liveliness and a directness she liked. For her own amusement, she sat at the dressing table and inked them. But she still seethed with restlessness and felt trapped.

She realized she needed fresh air and oceans of space, the solace of the limitless night. She rose and peered suspiciously out the window. Dr. Hyde-Crippen's light was out, and she hoped that meant he was safely in dreamland. She didn't want to take the chance of encountering him and his magic fingers outside in the darkness.

After supper she'd changed into a set of clingy wine-colored silken lounging pajamas, a Christmas gift from her parents. She'd taken the beaded clip from her hair and let it fall free once more, a tumble of dark curls. She glanced at her image in the pier glass as she slipped on her sandals. The lounging pajamas had a deeply cut neck, but they were hardly immodest. More of her was covered up than when she had worn her shorts and halter this afternoon. She supposed it was perfectly decent garb, and besides, no one was about to see her anyway. Cora's light was out, too, and she hadn't seen Jake since the afternoon.

Quietly she left her room and made her way through the semidarkness downstairs and toward the patio doors. Cora always left a few small lights burning throughout the house, in concession to Jake's frequent nocturnal rambling.

She slid the patio doors open and stepped out into the deliciously fresh night air. Far below she could hear the faint tumbling of the river, restless under the starlight. The wind stirred in the pines and the oaks, and the crickets sang.

She sighed and belted the sash of her pajamas more tightly. At the far corners of the patio, torches flared fitfully in the breeze, casting strange shadows on the flagstones. She moved toward the lounger that Hyde-Crippen had stretched on earlier in the day. She wanted to lie back and simply stare up at the stars, thinking of nothing.

She sat and sighed again. The stars in Nebraska seemed enormous and close, as if she could reach up and touch them. She shook out her hair allowing the night breeze to flow through it.

As she ran her slim fingers through her curls, an unexpected hand gripped her lightly by the wrist. She looked up in dismay, hoping Hyde-Crippen hadn't crept up on her. But it was Jake, standing over her, his left hand extended to grasp hers.

"Wearing that unruly mop loose again, Moranti?" he asked, his voice lightly sarcastic. "You shouldn't. It hides your pretty profile. I can barely see your face."

She swallowed hard, wishing his touch didn't affect her so powerfully. She drew her hand away, and he didn't resist. He put his hand in his back pocket in the familiar gesture and stood, staring down at her.

He looked more handsome than usual, Toby thought distractedly. He wore a crisp white shirt, its sleeves rolled back to accommodate his lightweight cast. His slacks were dark and emphasized the cowboy leanness of his hips and the length of his legs. His hair glittered darkly gold in the torchlight, and shadows played intriguingly on his chiseled cheekbones.

Toby's heart fluttered nervously as he moved to sit down in the lounger next to hers. She had spent most of the day promising herself that she wouldn't let him have this intoxicating effect on her. One appearance, and all her promises lay shattered and powerless around her.

Jake's eyes met hers, and she cursed herself for the way that simple, unemotional look made her heart race even faster.

"Thank you for leasing the car," she said awkwardly, "It's really quite—"

"Don't mention it," he said, cutting her off in a tone of bored dismissal.

"I just wanted to say—" she began again, flustered, but the cold command of his glance silenced her. He made it clear he didn't wish to speak of the car and that he didn't want to be thanked.

Impossible man, she thought in frustration.

"Well, I like it very much," she said, refusing to let him bully her into silence. "Not that I expect you care."

He ignored her and stared up at the stars. "Of course, I care," he said. "You're a decent assistant. I never wanted an assistant, but you're—decent. I want you to be happy. Within reason, of course."

He reached into the pocket of his shirt and drew out a cigarette. He lit it with a gold lighter. For a few seconds, his face was gilded by the brief flame.

Toby stared at him in spite of herself. She lowered one brow and watched him suspiciously as he exhaled. "I thought smoking was forbidden around here," she said, an edge of accusation in her voice.

"It is," he said, still not looking at her. "Because I'm trying to quit."

She leaned back against the lounger impatiently. "Really," she said shortly. "Nobody can smoke because you're trying to quit?"

"What do you care?" he asked lazily. "You don't smoke. And Cora never did. What difference does it make?"

"It's just that it's so—" She stopped. She had been going to say "high-handed," but realized how tasteless that would be. "It's so tyrannical—and typical." She turned her nose up to show him how typical and tyrannical it seemed.

He gave a joyless laugh. "Don't be an idiot. I have the right to control my own working environment—my own house, for God's sake. The only one it might affect is Hyde-Crippen, and he does his smoking on the sly anyway."

Toby turned abruptly to face him, but he was still studying the stars and ignoring her. "You know Hyde-Crippen smokes? Doesn't that make you suspicious of him?"

He tossed her the briefest of glances. "Of course I know. Why should it make me suspicious?"

"Because," Toby said logically, "it shows he doesn't practice what he preaches—that he isn't honest."

"A lot of people preach better than they practice," he shrugged. "A lot of extremely gifted people have extremely serious flaws."

Toby fought down the desire to glare at him righteously and utter, "You can say that again."

He looked at her and gave her a one-sided smile. "I, of course, have no flaws—except this." He held up the half-smoked cigarette. "And I'm giving it up."

"And doing a really wonderful job of it," Toby said sarcastically, watching him draw the smoke deeply into his lungs.

"This is the first one in six and a half weeks," he said, his voice bored again. "I haven't had one since—" He broke off. "For a long time," he amended, staring up at the stars again.

Toby bit her lip painfully. She knew what happened six and a half weeks ago—he was in the hospital and had learned just how badly injured his hand was.

"So what's the occasion?" she asked with false lightness. "Or do you just lapse with regularity, every six and a half weeks?"

"Ahh," he said, grinding out the cigarette in an enameled coaster. "The occasion is you, Moranti. What else could drive me to such degradation?"

"Me?" she asked, her heart starting to hammer again beneath the silk of her pajamas.

"You." He gave her a sideways, measuring look. "It seems I'm stuck with you—for a while—and that I'd better admit it. Isn't that sufficient to drive a man to vice?"

She didn't like the amused superiority glittering in his eyes. How, she wondered, could he be capable of upsetting her so effortlessly—and so completely? "Perhaps a man of stronger moral fiber wouldn't break down so easily," she said, giving him a dark look.

For the first time since she'd known him, he actually laughed. She was surprised that he had a warm, almost chuckling laugh. "Touché, Moranti," he said. "You're sharper than I'd expected—coming from that ungodly dull 'Dr. Dimbulb' strip."

"We prefer to call it 'Dr. Dimwit,'" she said in the same clipped tone. "It's a kind of tradition with us."

He gave that same startlingly warm laugh again. "I'm glad you don't take that dismal do-gooder seriously. How did you ever end up working on that old chestnut?"

"Tradition again," Toby said moodily. Although she and her co-workers had made fun of "Dr. Dinsmore" thousands of times, mockery from an outsider, especially Jake, was disturbing. After all, her parents had spent most of their professional lives working for Fantod Studios. "It's nothing that would interest you," she added defensively.

He looked bored, distant, again. "Probably not," he agreed. "What does interest me is why you're sitting out here with your neckline plunging and your hair loose. Hoping Hyde-Crippen will come along and kiss your foot again?"

His gaze traveled with insolent slowness over the neckline of her lounging pajamas, and she put one hand over her cleavage in self-defense, then felt prudish and childlike for doing so. She refused to dignify his accusation with a reply.

He smiled his crooked smile again. "That's what women like, isn't it? Somebody who'll kiss their feet? I myself always thought there were more interesting parts of a woman's anatomy to caress, but—"

"Oh, stop it!" Toby said. Embarrassed, she didn't move her hand from her neckline. "I don't like Dr. Hyde-Crippen, and I don't care about your amatory preferences."

"Maybe," he said smoothly, "it's because you don't know enough about either."

Again he was making her feel dizzy and disoriented. *Stop feeling this way,* she told herself desperately. The conversation was taking a path that led straight to the bedroom. She'd feared that Jake might try to lead her there when she had decided to stay on, and had vowed to avoid any advances. No man had ever affected her so physically and emotionally, and she resented the power it gave him.

She stood up abruptly, tightening her sash. "Good night, Mr. Ulrick," she said hurriedly, not looking at him. "I'll see you in the morning. At exactly seven o'clock."

She hoped she had sounded businesslike, but she doubted it. She was alarmed when he too stood, so swiftly that he blocked her path. For an insane moment she thought it might be both easy and inevitable to melt against him, put her arms around his neck, let him take her and the darkness take them both.

"Good night to you, too," he murmured. "And here's a helpful hint. If you don't want trouble, don't go lounging about men's patios at night in your sexy pajamas."

"They are not," she said, fighting to control her voice, "sexy."

"Aren't they?" he asked. She couldn't see his face in the shadows, but his tone was taunting. "Why, Miss Moranti—the only thing that stands between me and your considerable charms is this."

He took one end of her sash and fingered it, his touch faintly rustling the silk. "And this is a simple slip knot," he said, giving the sash the faintest of tugs. "One good pull, and I could unveil you like a statue."

She stood, helpless as if she were indeed a statue. She looked up at him. She wondered if he could see her heart beating through the thin silk. With only the flickering torchlight behind him, he looked like a man of darkness, ringed with fire.

"Don't—" she said softly, a note of pleading in her voice.

He laughed briefly. He dropped the end of the sash. "It's all right," he said. "I don't actually have to do it. I have an excellent imagination. I'll let it play—for a while. After all, anticipation is half the pleasure."

Frightened by him and by her own warring urges, Toby turned on her heel and fled. He was a complicated man with a complicated past, a chaotic present, an uncertain future. She didn't dare respond to him the way she wanted to.

The next morning, he was as remote, critical, and hard-driving as ever. He acted as if nothing had happened between them. She did, too. Gratefully, she lost herself in the escape of overwork.

CHAPTER SIX

JAKE PACED restlessly through the studio, and Toby sat at the drawing board, flexing her fingers ineffectually to release her rising tension.

Halfway through a new episode of "Heartland," Jake had decided the jokes needed strengthening. The story line centered on the efforts of Matilda's landlady, Mrs. Assettabee, to lose weight. In the original version, Mrs. Assettabee threw herself into calisthenics to the point of insanity.

At first Jake hadn't liked Toby's rendition of Mrs. Assettabee's exercise togs. When Toby finally did the drawing to his satisfaction, he decided he hated the whole idea. Toby groaned in frustration. He prowled the studio, restless as a caged wolf.

"I was too taken by the idea of her in those leg warmers, getting into those crazy aerobic positions," he grumbled. "It's a one-joke idea—it's boring. We'll have to change it."

"Maybe," Toby had offered, "she could go on an all-lettuce diet and start having nightmares about being a giant rabbit?" She quickly roughed a sketch of Mrs. Assettabee with rabbit ears, but Jake stared at it with disdain.

"Leave the narrative to me, will you, Moranti?" he asked sarcastically. "You're not a story-line person. You're an artist. On your good days."

"Well, ex-cuuuse me!" Toby said, hurt and angered. Every time she made a suggestion, he slapped it down as if it were a disease-bearing insect. Now she sat in silence, waiting for him to come up with something as the minutes ticked away.

"Okay," he said at last. "Let's make her a jogger. The idea has more potential. Sketch me Mrs. Assettabee in running gear."

He moved to stand towering behind her as her pencil whisked away.

"Baggy shorts—good," he mused, reaching over her shoulder and tapping the drawing. "Socks uneven—good. The way her shirt hangs—good. Put a sweatband on her forehead. Ahh. Tip it a little—like this." He picked up a pencil with his left hand and made a surprisingly firm line across the character's forehead. The line's placement was nearly perfect. Only the slightest unsteadiness revealed he had made it with his left hand.

But he saw that unsteadiness and despised it. "Damn!" he said viciously between his teeth. Toby stared down at the slightly imperfect line. She could feel his anger and unhappiness as he looked at it.

She had an abrupt intuitive flash. No ordinary right-handed person could have drawn so sure a line with the left hand. He was practicing using his left hand. He had to be. That must be one of the reasons he always stayed up so late—he was forcing his weaker hand to learn to do his will. His faith in Hyde-Crippen's ability to restore his right hand must not be complete, after all. He must know that he might never use it again.

He turned from the drawing board. "Draw it," he said bitterly. Her own anger had evaporated. Silently she drew the line of the headband, with the perfect control that he no longer had.

Out of the corner of her eye, she stole a quick glance at him. He was staring out the windows into the middle distance, and she could see the rage and the determination in his face. A muscle jumped in his cheek.

Then he glanced at her and was his old self. "Hurry up, Moranti," he said coldly. "I don't pay you to dawdle. Draw, will you?" His tone was brusque, emotionless.

Quickly she turned to her work, her throat constricted. She felt, for the briefest of moments, she had at last glimpsed the depth of the emotion surging within him.

That glimpse of the war Jake fought within himself haunted Toby the rest of the day. When he went off for his afternoon session with Hyde-Crippen, Toby took a coffee break with Cora. "He's practicing using his left hand," she told Cora. "I know he is. He's driving himself terribly hard; he scares me."

"He's always driven himself hard," Cora said, but she looked troubled at the news. "But maybe there's a bright side to this. It means he can't really believe that crazy Hyde-Crippen can actually do anything. But it'd take him years to get the control in his left hand he had in his right."

That was depressingly true, and Toby knew it. Suddenly, in spite of all common sense, she wanted to believe in Hyde-Crippen. She wanted the ridiculous little man to prove to be a Merlin, a wise wizard disguised as a fool. She wanted, more than anything, for him to restore the magic to Jake's right hand.

"Look," Toby said, staring at Cora's dubious face, "how do we know Hyde-Crippen can't do any good? Jake's not stupid. He wouldn't put himself through all this if there weren't some chance—"

"Jake's stubborn," Cora said, unconvinced. "He doesn't give up easy. If he fails at anything, he thinks it's because he didn't try hard enough. If he can't do it one way, he'll try another, and he'll keep trying till he drops. That's his blessing—and his curse."

Toby gloomily studied her coffee cup, as if it contained an evil fortune. "What exactly did these other doctors say?" she probed, looking for any crumb of hope.

Cora gave her an unfathomable black glance. "Three said he'd probably never use the hand again. One of them in fact wanted to amputate—he said the discoloration looked dangerous. One said it looked hopeless, but miracles sometimes happen."

"Isn't it possible Hyde-Crippen is the miracle?" Toby offered hopefully. "I know he's ludicrous and conceited and comes off as a snake oil salesman—but he must know something, surely?"

"Yeah," Cora said bitterly, finishing her coffee. "He knows how to sell hope when there's none available."

"You're sure?" Toby pursued. "Why? At least one doctor said there was a possibility—"

Cora sighed, rose and refilled her coffee cup. "Toby, they have this machine at the hospital. It measures the electricity going through the nerves. That's what the energy in nerves is—a kind of electricity. When they measured the impulses in Jake's hand, there was nothing—a blank. Three doctors—three good doctors—said that meant the nerves were destroyed. A fourth said there was an outside chance they weren't. But it was a long shot."

"A chance how far outside? A shot how long?"

"I'm no doctor," Cora said wearily, sitting down again. "The way I understand it is this: the nerves to the hand go through these tunnels of bone in the wrist. There's a possibility—faint—that the nerves are simply so swollen they've jammed up the tunnels, like a traffic jam. Nothing can get through. One doctor said it was a possibility. Hyde-Crippen claims that's what happened. That the feeling and control can be restored—but only, of course, by him."

"Well," Toby asked doggedly, "isn't there a possibility he's right? Maybe that's the case."

"Oh, come on, Toby," Cora said, almost irritably. "Who could prove it either way? You can't X-ray a nerve. And if he was right, there should be improvement by now—if anything Jake's worse. He's in more pain than when he came home from the hospital. He doesn't say anything, but I can tell. Hyde-Crippen's telling Jake precisely what Jake wants to believe. You've heard him talk—nonsense, that's all. If he isn't a fraud, he's a nut case."

"But Jake's not easily fooled," Toby protested. "How did he find Hyde-Crippen—how did he get involved with him?"

"Pah!" Cora said in disgust. "Hyde-Crippen found him. The next thing I know, Jake has him living with us and pulling his crazy hocus-pocus. At a fee you wouldn't believe, I might add."

Toby sighed and stared down at the checkered tablecloth. "Still," she said meditatively, "Jake might not be completely wrong . . . but if he's going through all this, and trying to use his left hand at the same time, it's too much."

Cora set down her cup and looked at her. Her eyes were hard with warning, but the line of her mouth was sad. "Look, kid," she said, "I understand why you'd like to believe Hyde-Crippen can do what he says. But don't fall for that delusion at this stage of the game. The chances are ninety-nine percent Jake'll never use that hand again. If he's practicing with his left hand, it means he's starting to accept the facts. And everybody with any sense knows that's exactly what he has to do—accept it. It's going to take him a long time. You really don't want him hanging on to false hopes, do you?"

And for that, Toby could think of no answer.

THAT AFTERNOON, her ever-shifting sympathies took another violent change of direction. Jake returned from his session with Hyde-Crippen in obvious pain. He looked tired, and she realized he needed sleep. Again she wondered how hard he was driving himself and how long he could keep it up.

The changes they were making in the Mrs. Assettabee episode put him in a more dangerous mood than usual, and his criticisms were especially barbed. He kept her working until almost eleven o'clock that night.

"Would you tell me one thing?" she challenged when he finally told her to go. "Do you always work at this pace?"

He glanced at her coldly. "The accident put me behind."

"But we're catching up fast," Toby remonstrated. "Heartland is already ahead of schedule as much as some strips. Shouldn't you slow down?"

"What's the matter? Can't take it?" he asked with a tight smile.

"I can take it," she replied, struggling to keep her voice even. "I just wonder what the point is."

"The point," he said, standing by the window and staring out into the darkness, "is I like being ahead. Then I can knock off for two months in the winter. Go to Hawaii. Recharge my batteries."

"Hawaii?" Toby practically wailed. "I'm working myself to death so you can go to Hawaii and sun yourself on the sand like a lizard?"

"Don't knock it," he tossed back, his tone bored. "You've never gone through a Nebraska winter."

"And what am I supposed to do when you're in Hawaii?" she demanded. "Go back to Jersey? Stay here and feed your horse? Or follow along and wax your surfboard?"

He turned to look at her. He hid a yawn behind his gloved hand. "Frankly, I haven't given it any thought. Maybe I'll bring you along for company. Cora never comes. She hates planes, loathes pineapple, and looking at waves makes her seasick. You're probably cute in a sarong. You can stand beside my hammock and fan me."

"Stop teasing." She tossed her head impatiently. "I mean it. What am I supposed to do when you go to Hawaii? I never knew about this."

He turned his back and stared out into the night again. "I haven't bothered to think that far ahead. And neither should you. I'll see when the time comes. Go to bed, Moranti."

HER NERVES WERE too tightly wound for her to even think of sleeping. Angrily, looking for some way to vent her frustration, she spied the satiric drawings she had done of Jake as the ultimate egocentric artist. On impulse, she slipped them into a large envelope and addressed them to the cartoon editor of *City Lights, The Magazine of Manhattan.* *City Lights* was one of the most prestigious magazines in the country, and it ran only the finest cartoons. She knew they would reject her, but she didn't care. It was a way to strike out at Jake, however impotently. *Hawaii,* she thought with disgust. And he hadn't bothered to think about what he was going to do about her. And what did he mean that she shouldn't think that far ahead? Did he assume she'd be gone by the winter? Would she be?

Before she could change her mind, she went downstairs, walked outside and got into the Mustang. She drove into Zion Bluff and dropped the envelope into the mailbox outside the little white clapboard post office. It was, she realized with irony, the first time she'd driven the Mustang since she'd brought it home.

It was typical, she fumed, negotiating the dark and curving road back to the house; he was driving her like a slave so he could go off and lounge on a beach for two months. And he hadn't bothered to give so much as a thought to what she might be doing then.

But when she returned to the house, she saw the lights blazing in the other tower room—Jake's room. She knew he was up there, alone and probably exhausted, forcing himself to learn to draw again with his left hand.

Suddenly she felt overwhelmed with admiration and hope for him, and pricked with worry. She was also deeply ashamed of herself for letting him anger her. She went to bed. She awoke once in the earliest hours of the morning. She sat up sleepily and looked out the east windows. Jake's light still shone stubbornly through the darkness.

THE NEXT MORNING, while Hyde-Crippen worked his voodoo rites on Jake's hand, Toby went into the kitchen for coffee and information.

"What's this about Hawaii?" she asked, filling her cup.

"Hawaii?" Cora asked, eyebrows rising. "Is he talking about going to Hawaii? It's news to me—"

"He says he always goes," Toby answered, sitting down and rubbing the back of her neck.

"He does," shrugged Cora with a slight frown. "In February and March. I just thought that this winter—well, he wouldn't."

"He said that's why he was working so hard."

Cora gave a derisive snort. "He always works hard. Hawaii, eh? I wonder if that means he thinks he'll be done with Hyde-Crippen by then."

"Probably." Toby stared moodily into her coffee. *And me, too,* she thought. *He can't wait to be done with me.*

Cora watched her carefully. "I wouldn't count on him going anywhere, Toby," she said at last. "It's just one more wild dream he's got that everything's going to be the way it was. Well, it's not. He's got to adjust to that."

But he won't adjust, Toby thought. Never. Not him. Her eyes met Cora's and held them. They both knew it.

That night, after supper, when Jake disappeared with Hyde-Crippen for an extra session and Cora was having one of her lengthy telephone conversations with the mysterious Herbert, Toby sat on the patio and tried to write to Hank and Ralph and Lawrence at Fantod Studios.

But the letter, like most she managed to scribble nowadays, said nothing. It seemed hollow, empty, false. She knew it was because what was foremost in her mind was what she did not dare commit to paper: the depth and complexity of her feelings about Jake. She hated admitting those feelings even to herself.

The next two weeks did nothing to simplify her emotions. Jake made her reactions to him see-saw madly. Resentment alternated with admiration. She experienced moments when she couldn't understand him at all and moments when she seemed to understand him perfectly.

Once, going through an old file of sketches, she found a drawing wedged in the back of the drawer. The paper was yellowed, and the work was unlike any of his she had seen before. It was a picture of a blond girl of surpassing beauty. Her long hair fell across her face, almost obscuring one haunting eye. "Denise," it said at the bottom, "I'll love you forever." So this was Denise, she thought unhappily, studying the sketch. It was a face she supposed a man could love forever.

But then she looked more closely. The picture was very old. The style was very much like Jake's, yet with a subtle difference she couldn't quite pinpoint. Perhaps Raynor had done it, she thought with a sudden swell of hope. Then she wondered what was wrong with her and thrust the sketch back where she found it. What did it matter if Jake hadn't drawn it? Why should the possibility give her such a ludicrous surge of joy? It was ridiculous. She began to think if she didn't have better sense, she might be falling in love with the man.

"A DAY OFF?" Toby said, her brown eyes wide with disbelief. She looked across the supper table at Cora. "You're kidding me, aren't you? This is some cruel trick. We're not really taking a day off...are we?"

Cora smiled. She'd been working on Jake's business accounts, and still had on her half-moon reading glasses. Somehow they seemed to go perfectly with her braids and beaded necklace. "I do not speak with forked tongue. All day Saturday—off. Saturday night, too. Stop grinning so wide—the sparkle is hurting my eyes.''

Dr. Hyde-Crippen, mixing small pieces of boiled parsnip with his brown rice, cleared his throat. "I like to think this unexpected holiday is due to my influence," he said with self-satisfaction. "I've insisted—for Miss Moranti's sake as well as his own—that Mr. Ulrick take off a bit more time to relax. And so, tomorrow, he's doing so—on the counsel of his physician."

Cora gave him a withering look. "Tomorrow is Founder's Day," she said, her mouth sardonic. "It's the Old Settler's Picnic, the Community Sing, the Square Dance and the Carnival. We never miss Founder's Day. Jake picks up a lot of ideas for the strip there."

"Ummph," said Hyde-Crippen uncomfortably, his mouth full.

"You'll love it," she told him darkly. "It's a junk-food jamboree. You can hide behind a tree and snarf corn dogs and cotton candy to your heart's content."

Hyde-Crippen started to retort, but instead choked on his parsnips and turned scarlet.

Cora pounded on his back as if it gave her infinite satisfaction.

Toby awoke slowly and blissfully on Saturday morning. Her sheets were silk, a fact she'd hardly had time to appreciate, and she stretched out luxuriously in them—a whole extra day off! She was going to spend it doing everything— and nothing. She'd take a long bubble bath, wash her hair, sun herself on the patio, write some real letters and work on "Taffy."

"Umm," she said, and stretched again, smiling at the sunshine that fell through the windows of her tower room. Then she stopped smiling. Something was different in the house. She frowned.

Music—very loud music—was coming from the kitchen. And it was not Cora's music. It was rock music—the Rolling Stones, in fact. Puzzled, Toby jumped from bed, donned her jeans, favorite pink summer sweater and pink jogging shoes. She pinned her hair back with Cora's clip and put on a touch of lip gloss.

Taking the steps two at a time, she bounded downstairs to investigate. The smell of freshly perked coffee greeted her when she reached the ground floor and the scent of bacon and eggs drew her on like a magic spell.

But she stopped short when she reached the kitchen. Jake stood by the stove, scrambling eggs. He had an outsize portable cassette player on the counter, from which the Stones were blaring. He was obviously enjoying the music, even swinging his hips to it; he swung them very well, Toby noted nervously, and he was singing along—"I can't get no—no-oo sa-tis-fac-tion. . . ."

He turned, saw her and gave her a crooked grin. He began to move toward her with that same snake-hipped and frankly sexy grace. His startling blue eyes met her dark ones. He had the spatula in his left hand and a dish towel fastened around his lean waist in lieu of an apron.

Toby took a step backward involuntarily. "Where's Cora?" she asked apprehensively. "And what's got into you? Or is this how you always celebrate Founder's Day, dancing lewdly with a spatula?"

"Oh," he said, in his lowest voice, "The spatula makes you nervous? I'll get rid of it." He flung it cavalierly to the sink. "Apron makes you nervous? I'll do a strip tease."

He untied the apron and let it sink to the floor. "Now," he said, advancing on her again. "What's to stand between us? Come here, my raven-haired beauty."

He cornered her against the cabinets and put his left arm around her waist. Toby flinched, not knowing whether to laugh or try to run. She couldn't believe the way he was acting. What had got into him? "Where's Cora?" she demanded again. But he was pulling her provocatively close and forcing her to dance. "Let's spend the night together," he sang in her ear, in perfect harmony with the tape.

He danced wonderfully, Toby noticed with dismay, and he held her very, very close. He smiled down at her, his usual slanted, mocking smile. "Um," he said softly. "You're a nice little armful, Moranti. Just the right size."

Her perfidious heart leaped up at his unexpected nearness, and her senses whirled, threatening to go out of control. *Stop this,* she ordered herself in rising panic, watching the curve of his sensual mouth in fascination.

"Your eggs are burning," she said stiffly.

He released her with an immediacy that was almost disappointing. "Oop," he said, as if he'd already forgotten he'd just held her and sung suggestively in her ear. "Our breakfast."

"Our breakfast?" Toby demanded, trying to regain control of her thoughts. What had got into Jake? she wondered. "What do you mean, our breakfast? And where's Cora?"

"What I mean by our breakfast is our breakfast," he said matter-of-factly. "Cora's gone into town with her swain. Sit down. I scramble a mean egg. I perk a powerful coffee. I sizzle a succulent bacon."

Reluctantly she sat as he filled a plate for her. He had to work with his left hand, but he moved with surprising efficiency and confidence. "Cora has a swain?" she asked, watching him, perplexed by this sudden garrulous streak. "A boyfriend? She never said anything. Who is he?"

He set a plate before her. "Cora hardly ever talks about her private life," he said sardonically. "She'd rather talk about mine. His name is Herbert Olssen. He's a farmer, and he's been after her for years. Five, in fact."

He filled his own plate and sat across from her.

So that explained Herbert, she thought. "If he's so devoted, why hasn't he been around?" she asked. She tasted her eggs. Jake was, indeed, a tolerable cook.

"You don't know much about farming," he answered, a hint of scorn in his voice. "Herb works sunup to sundown every day till after harvest. Then he'll be lounging around the kitchen trying to get Cora to break down and marry him."

"So why doesn't she?" Toby asked, "Or is all the ardor on his side?"

Jake frowned and shook his head. "She likes him all right. But she's a stubborn lady. She wants him to quit farming and go back to teaching, which is his first love. Cora's a great believer in education. She's got two degrees herself, you know. And still takes night classes."

"She does?" Toby asked, surprised she'd never mentioned it.

"Cora goes to school more than anybody I know," Jake replied, darting her a satiric look. "When Empire Features picked up on my strip, I asked her what she wanted most in the world. I'd buy it for her. Well, she wanted an education. So she took night classes till she got a B.A., and then she got an M.B.A., and last fall she started taking classes in contract law."

"She's an amazing woman," Toby said in admiration. "Poor Mr. Olssen may have a tough time landing her."

"Don't be so sure," he corrected. "Herbert's just about ready to put the farm up for sale. Cora's right—he really was cut out to teach, not to farm. Of course, I could speed things up for them—all I'd have to do is get married."

Toby almost choked on her toast. "Married?" she asked, clearing her throat and taking a quick sip of coffee.

"She says the day I get married, she's going to be out of here like a shot. She's known me too long. She'd be too much like a mother-in-law. Oh, she'd still take care of my accounts and business stuff. But I'd have to find another housekeeper."

"But you, I suppose, are completely above any such middle-class arrangements as marriage," Toby offered airily, trying to sound disinterested.

His face hardened. "I thought about it once. I was a damned fool," he said acidly. "I won't ever think about it again, I guarantee you. Hell will freeze first."

He sounded bitter. She feared he had never really recovered from his ill-fated engagement to Denise, and she wished she had said nothing at all. "That's rather unfortunate for Herbert," she replied, staring down at her plate.

"Ha," he scoffed. "Herbert will get her anyway. And Cora will get him back to where he belongs—in the classroom. He knows she's right. And she realizes more all the time just how good a man he is.

"But let's not talk of marriages," he said wryly. "Bad for the digestion. Clean up your plate, curly locks. Let's get going."

"Going? Going where?" Toby asked, still wondering if his harsh words disguised an undimmed flame of emotion for Denise. He was still such an intense man, she suspected it was so.

"Goin'?" he asked, in his best imitation of an innocent rustic. "Why, woman, we're goin' to *town*. It's Founder's Day. Biggest dag-nabbed celebration we got in these parts."

Toby pushed her plate away and shook her head. "Oh, no," she said as firmly as she could. "None of my ancestors founded anything around here, and it's my day off. I'm not going to do anything but lie in the sun and rest."

"Wrong," he corrected implacably. "It's my day off. It's Cora's day off. But at the salary I pay you, it's not your day off. Sunday is. So you're coming with me."

"No," Toby wailed, wondering what he was trying to do to her now. "Why? It's not fair!"

"Because I need you." He said it sardonically, but the words made her heart stumble, then soar momentarily.

"I need you for two purposes," he continued, his eyebrow cocked in mock patience. "One, to help me with the kids. Two, to help me with the women."

"What kids? What women? Help you how?" she asked, eyeing him suspiciously.

"You'll see," he said laconically. "Besides, you need to get to know Zion Bluff. You've been drawing life in the Midwest. It's about time you saw some of it."

"Then I'll have to change clothes," she said, sighing wearily. "And put on my makeup."

"Your clothes look fine," he said, his gaze flicking over the pink sweater with cool interest. "And you don't need makeup, Moranti. Don't you know that? It's gilding the lily. You've got the face of a beauty out of a Renaissance painting. You can't enhance it. It's practically perfect the way it is."

She blushed and looked away. The compliment was so unexpected she didn't know how to deal with it. She could think of no answer, and found herself muttering, "I wish you wouldn't always call me Moranti."

He reached across the table and put his fingers lightly on her chin, turning her face to his. He looked at her, his blue eyes unreadable and hard. "But it's so much safer for us both if I do, Moranti," he said with false lightness. "Haven't you figured that out yet?"

Her senses tumbled in confusion. Again she was haunted by the feeling that sometimes she understood him completely—and sometimes, as now, she felt she knew nothing about him at all—and that was probably exactly how he wanted it.

Yet when, still touching her face, he gave her the slightest of smiles, she couldn't help smiling back. This morning was the first time she had seen him in a truly good mood. Why that so sincerely gladdened her heart, she could not say.

CHAPTER SEVEN

TOBY WAS UNSETTLED even more when Jake insisted they ride the flashy big pinto, Tango, into town. "The kids in town like him," Jake said firmly. "Tango's a lot bigger celebrity to them than I am."

"I can't ride a horse," Toby said in horror. The closest she had ever come to riding was on a pony in the park as a child. Worst of all, Jake wasn't going to use a saddle; he expected her to ride behind him bareback.

"All you have to do is hang on to me," he grumbled, helping her clamber up onto the horse's broad back. And when he started out at a bone-shaking trot, Toby found herself slipping and sliding wildly. If she had to cling to Jake any tighter she was certain she'd crack his ribs.

"Slow down," she begged. "This horse has more hip movements than a hula dancer! I'm bouncing all over."

"Just relax," he laughed, and kicked the horse into a faster trot. She hung onto Jake so hard she felt as if she was going to merge into his body and become a part of him. He laughed again, enjoying himself more than he had any right to.

The little town of Zion Bluff was hardly recognizable when Toby and Jake approached it on the dancing, head-tossing pinto. The normally somnolent little park was a sea of milling adults, running children and strolling clowns selling balloons and popcorn. At the band shell, an enthusiastic bluegrass band wailed out a spirited version of "Darlin' Cory."

To the east of the park, streets were blocked off to accommodate booths for those selling arts and crafts, and for two of the day's ongoing and most popular events: the chili cook-off and the corn boil.

Large homemade signs in red, white and blue announced that the carnival would glitter all day and all evening at the Zion Bluff fairgrounds and that night there would be square dancing, the crowning of Miss Pioneer Spirit of Zion Bluff, then a rodeo followed by a fireworks display.

Toby was enchanted by the enthusiastic grassroots celebration, though she would have been more so if she were not so dazed from the jolting ride on that high-stepping pinto. When Jake helped her down, she felt weak, rubbery-kneed and bowlegged. She swayed a bit, and Jake's left arm shot out to steady her. His touch was more debilitating than the ride, but she was too weak to extricate herself. She let him guide her toward the craft displays, his left arm intimately wound around her slim waist.

"Come on," he teased, his breath warm against her ear. "It wasn't that bad was it?"

"I have a new respect for those TV models that go galloping off through the wildflowers on the white stallion," Toby said shakily. "Their bottoms must be made of iron." She touched the seat of her jeans gingerly.

"You lost your hair clip," he said, laughing. "Poor Tango. He's got a relatively smooth gait. I'd hate to see how you'd do on a really rough-gaited horse."

She put her hand up to her hair in dismay. The clip must have fallen out along the road, and her curly hair spilled loosely down her back. Hurriedly, she tried to smooth it into order. She knew Jake preferred it pulled back, though why should that matter?

"We'll fix you up." He grinned. "Look over there—just what we need." He nodded toward one of the arts and crafts booths, draped with red, white and blue bunting and displaying a wealth of silver jewelry.

"Hello, Knut," Jake said, greeting the booth's proprietor, a lean, weathered, elderly man in overalls and a wide straw hat. "The lady lost her hair clip. What have you got in the way of replacements?"

"Hey, Jake. How's the hand?" the man replied. He said it gruffly, and in such a rush that the sentences came out as one long, low, shy word.

"Hand's great," Jake replied pleasantly, "and this is my new assistant, Toby Moranti—Toby, meet Knut Hansen. A fine farmer, but a great silversmith."

Knut, not looking at Toby, nodded bashfully as he pushed a tray of silver hair clips across the narrow counter.

Although the clips were beautiful and finely wrought, and many were set with turquoise, malachite or polished agate, she hardly saw them. She was staring in surprise at Jake. *Where,* she thought in perplexity, *has this charming, friendly fellow suddenly come from?*

"Take your pick, Toby," Jake instructed, his arm still around her waist. "He's one of the best native craftsmen around. Tiffany's lost a hell of a silversmith when Knut decided to keep on farming."

He squeezed her a bit more tightly, and Toby swallowed hard, trying to sort out her emotions. Now he was actually calling her by her first name—treating her with affection and even respect. Nothing could have seemed more out of character.

Automatically she pointed to the most modest of the silver barrettes, but Jake shook his head and picked out three of the most beautiful. "We'll take those," he instructed. He picked up the one wrought in an abstract design set with brilliant green malachite. "Here," he said, handing it to her. "I'll help you."

He gathered her hair gently at the nape of the neck. "You don't have to," she said nervously. Her fingers could not help brushing his, and the touch made her nerves quiver. "And you don't have to buy me anything."

"I like touching your hair," he said, his voice low. "It's like holding a handful of silk. And I'll buy you things if I want to—maybe it'll make up for you not having a day off."

Knut Hansen wrapped the other two pieces in tissue and put them in a small paper bag. "Thank you," Toby said softly, when he gave them to her. "You do beautiful work."

The man seemed to go redder under his sunburn, still refused to meet her eyes and made a strangled uncomfortable sound deep in his throat.

"Is he always that shy?" Toby asked, as Jake led her away.

"No," Jake said lightly. He had put his hand back on the curve of her waist again. "He's usually much shyer. He was practically loquacious today. Doesn't he remind you of anybody?"

Toby looked up at him in puzzlement. Then comprehension dawned in her eyes. "You based a character in 'Heartland' on him," she accused, her lips parted in disbelief. "Knut Hansen is Bashful Skitterman, isn't he? The farmer who's so shy he only speaks once a year?"

Jake nodded. "In the holiday strip he's always hiding down in the corner, saying 'Merry Christmas' in tiny letters. Yep, Bashful's based on old Knut, all right."

"Goodness," Toby asked, still unsure whether to laugh or be aghast, "doesn't he know? Doesn't he care?"

"People never guess." Jake shrugged. "They never recognize themselves. Besides, he isn't really Bashful Skitterman—he just inspired him. Oh, some people suspect their neighbors are in the strip. I think secretly they like the idea. It makes Zion Bluff a bit special."

Toby looked at the crowd with new alertness. "You mean the characters in 'Heartland' are based on people here?"

He smiled down crookedly. "Vaguely—the characters in the strip are exaggerated beyond proportion—and usually beyond recognition. That's another reason I brought you today—it's an intelligence test, curly locks. You know the characters. Now let's see if you can spot the originals—or if I've disguised them cleverly enough."

Toby raised her chin and smiled at the challenge. In spite of herself, she was also smiling at Jake, for he seemed a different person today—cheerful, even playful. By noon, she impressed him by spotting more than a dozen natives of Zion Bluff who had metamorphosed into major characters in "Heartland."

"You're pretty good at this," he muttered ruefully after she correctly guessed a dark-clad, dour man had partially inspired the humorless character of Judge McChoakum.

"I'd only expect you to hire the best, Mr. Ulrick," she teased.

He merely gave her the sideways smile that made her heart flutter like the wings of a fledgling learning to fly.

She also discovered what Jake had meant by bringing her along to deal with the children and women.

The children had been after him almost as soon as they noticed he was there. He had a surprising rapport with them.

"Jake! Did you ride Tango in? Will you make him do his tricks?"

"Jake! I'm gonna be an artist, too, when I grow up!"

"You gonna ride Tango at the rodeo?"

"Your hand okay, Jake?"

"Draw me a Matilda, Jake. Will ya, huh?"

"Yeah, draw me one, too—and one for my cousin in Chicago—please, Jake?"

Jake showed surprising patience and good humor with them. "Tango's tethered over in the shade and anybody who tries to get on him gets a personal paddling from me. I'm not riding him at the rodeo this year, but we'll make it up next year. Yes, my hand's going to be fine, but if you want any pictures of Matilda, ask the pretty lady. She's doing the drawing until I can do it myself again."

At this last bit of news the children looked at Toby with frank suspicion. Who was she, they obviously wondered, and how did she think she could draw as well as their hero?

But shortly, as if to test her, they were shoving pieces of paper in her direction. She sat at the picnic table, Jake next to her, sketching picture after picture of Matilida—on napkins, paper plates, pieces ripped from bags—in short, anything that could be drawn upon.

"She's pretty good," said a tough-looking little red-headed boy, examining his drawing. "She's pretty near good as you, Jake."

"I think she *is* as good as you," a little blond girl said saucily, and climbed up to sit as close as possible beside Toby. "I didn't know ladies could be artists, too," she said, looking up at Toby as if she had just shifted her hero worship from Jake to Toby.

"Women can do just about anything they set their minds to nowadays," Toby told the girl and gave her a smile.

"Don't you care if she does your drawing?" asked another boy, who looked wise beyond his years. "I mean, she is just a girl."

Jake's arm was draped familiarly around Toby's shoulder. "She's my right-hand girl," he said amiably. "The best there is. But she's been drawing for you for nearly forty-five minutes. Let her enjoy the afternoon. Maybe she'll draw more for you while the square dance is going on tonight—if you're polite and if you behave."

Reluctantly the children scattered. Toby, her fingers aching from the swiftness with which she'd had to execute the drawings, looked wryly at Jake beside her on the picnic bench. "How do you manage that?" she asked, her mouth quirking in cynical amusement.

"Manage what?" he asked, the picture of affronted innocence.

"Manage to charm those children," she answered, her expression skeptical. "I'd have guessed you were the type

who kicked dogs and snarled at children. But those kids
adore you. How do you pull off that deception?''

"Ah," he said with mock cynicism. "I do have a way with
the little yard apes, don't I?"

"Yard apes!" Toby remonstrated. "See—you don't even
like them."

"Who said I didn't like them?" he asked mildly. "I like
them fine. They're a hell of a lot more honest than adults.
And I'm on their wavelength. You think a comic artist ever
dares to grow up completely? No way, Mona Lisa. I'm still
a little bit of a yard ape myself. And when I'm not, I'd better retire."

"Really," she said, shaking her head to clear it. The man
seemed more impossible all the time. Yet she had the
sneaking suspicion he could communicate with children
better than most adults could, and that he liked them better
than he liked adults.

As the afternoon ripened and she watched Jake among
the people of the town, a realization began to dawn: there
was a streak of shyness in Jake's nature. He was most comfortable with the children and with people who were either
quiet themselves, like Knut Hansen, or totally natural and
without pretention. With others, he adopted an aloof and
rather mocking persona. It was not rude, but neither was it
truly friendly. If anything, it was cleverly defensive.

She also saw what he meant about holding off the women.
Several of them laid sieges that made those of the children
seem insignificant. At times Toby felt Jake was using her to
make his way through a matrimonial mine field.

"Jake—sweety!" gurgled a blue-haired matron. "I want
you to meet my niece Elsie from Minneapolis. Elsie is a fine
arts major at the university. She'd just love to pick your
brain about her career options."

Jake smiled benignly at Mrs. Elofson, who had a multi-
tude of chins, and just as benignly at the eye-batting Elsie—who seemed to have no chin at all.

"Lovely niece—as lovely as yourself, Mrs. Elofson," he said smoothly. Then he patted Toby's hand, which he had tucked through his right arm. "But this little gal has been taking up all my time lately—have you met my assistant, Toby Moranti? If Toby ever has a spare afternoon, maybe she could give Elsie some advice. Toby's from the East and she knows much more about what opportunities are opening up. I'm sure you'd love to help Elsie out, wouldn't you, dear?"

Toby tried to keep her expression blank. *The fox,* she thought, eyeing the disappointed faces of Mrs. Elofson and the chinless Elsie. *The cunning golden fox.* Mrs. Elofson had obviously imported Elsie as a serious contender for the town's most eligible bachelor, and Jake had, with a few clever sentences, shot down all such heady hopes—and dumped the problem into Toby's lap as well.

"But you're so much more experienced than this—little thing," Mrs. Elofson flattered, making one last desperate attempt to win Jake's attention to the hapless Elsie.

"This little thing," Jake said, nuzzling Toby's cheek, "has taught me things I never knew, believe me, Mrs. Elofson."

"I'm sure she has," sniffed Mrs. Elofson, all her chins waggling in disapproval. "And I hope your hand is fine, Jake. Will you be needing your—assistant—much longer?"

"The hand is coming along nicely." Jake smiled blandly. "But who knows how long I'll ask this little beauty to stay on?"

"That was disgusting," Toby hissed, when Mrs. Elofson waddled off, Elsie in reluctant tow.

"I told you," he said, his gaze cool and hooded, "part of your job today is to keep these damned matchmakers off my back. Every summer half a dozen misguided women import their eligible relatives, then set them on me like hounds. I have a right to protect myself."

"Not by nuzzling on my cheek," Toby said hotly. "Not by giving me little squeezes and hugs. And not by implying I'm anything more than your assistant—"

"All's fair in love, war, and defending one's sacred bachelorhood," he answered with finality. "Ah—another salvo. Try to smile up at me and look adoring."

"How could I possibly adore you?" Toby whispered angrily, "you hypocrite—"

But his arm tightened around her waist, more in warning than affection.

This time it was a plump young woman, Mrs. Sparkman, who had a tower of teased blond hair, and wore pounds of eye makeup. She was dead set on introducing Jake to her recently divorced cousin, Cookie. Cookie was even plumper, wore even more makeup, had an even higher tower of peroxided hair and was stuffed provocatively into the tightest shorts Toby had ever seen.

Again Jake spoke as glowingly of Toby as if he had just proposed to her. He complimented her, blew one of her stray curls back into place, looked at her with appreciation practically flaming in his blue eyes. Mrs. Sparkman and Cookie, clearly outmaneuvered, quickly retreated.

"You," Toby said, "are the most mendacious man I've ever met—a really horrible humbug, do you know that?"

"Oh, hush," he said almost absently and pulled her a bit closer. He tried to blow the errant curl into place once again. "Did you really want me to leave you and go off with that walking sausage in the blond fright wig?"

"That's a terrible thing to say about a woman who's just trying to be friendly," Toby answered righteously.

"There's no more relentless creature on earth than a female with a marriageable friend or relative," he returned with equal righteousness. "And if I wanted a woman with hair taller than the World Trade Center, I'd look for her myself. I wouldn't be waiting for Anita Sparkman to hurl her into my lap. Oops—all systems on alert—I sense another one."

The next wave of attack was truly serious, and it was commanded by Mrs. Ekdahl, the banker's tall and stately wife. She cornered them just as Jake and Toby were about to enter the carnival midway. Mrs. Ekdahl was a well-preserved and perfectly poised woman who wore just enough diamonds to show she was rich, but not quite enough to actually be ostentatious. The stunning weapon she hoped to drop on Jake was her stepdaughter Marietta—home on vacation from New York.

Marietta was lovely. She was dressed in a cream-colored silk shift as expensive as it was sensuous. Her auburn hair was pulled back almost severely to accentuate the pert sexiness of her face. She had a charming retroussé nose, a pretty, pouty mouth, but a peculiarly vacant look in her eyes.

"Jake, darling," murmured Mrs. Ekdahl, patting his cheek. "How are you, darling? We've all been so concerned. Is this your little assistant we've all heard so much about? A little Italian girl, aren't you, dear?" she said, smiling brittlely at Toby. "I must have my maid get a recipe for spaghetti from you sometime. Jake, do you recognize my Marietta? You haven't seen her since she took up modeling in New York—it's been—what?—four long years."

Jake showed white teeth in an excellent imitation of a smile. "Who could forget Marietta?" he said genially, but his fingers were laced through Toby's, and absently, as if it were a habit he no longer thought about, he raised Toby's hand to his lips and kissed it.

Marietta's smile never faltered. It might have been pasted on. "I love modeling," she purred, then batted her vacant eyes at Jake's gloved hand. "But I want to do more with my life. I do volunteer work. I help the handicapped. It's my favorite job of all. I love to help crippled people."

Toby stiffened at Marietta's lack of tact, but Jake's charm never wavered. "That's what my little Toby's doing right now," he said, kissing her hand again. "Helping the handicapped. In this case, me. And a fine job she does of it. Extraordinary woman."

"But you will be well," Mrs. Ekdahl said icily. "Your little friend will be going back to her...oh...own kind soon, I suppose."

"I'll soon be fine," he replied warmly. "But poor Toby is an orphan child. Doesn't have a soul in the world. I may keep her on as an assistant permanently. Marvelous creature. Truly marvelous."

"I'm sure," said Mr. Ekdahl between her teeth. "Nevertheless, you must pry yourself from her sometime and come for supper while Marietta's home. Mustn't he, Marietta?"

"Oh, please," cooed Marietta at her most tempting.

"Sorry." Jake grinned, nuzzling Toby's neck. "Couldn't leave Toby's spaghetti. She's got me addicted."

With a minimum of grace, he excused himself and Toby, then nearly dragged her to the midway.

"Oh!" Toby sputtered, stumbling behind him. She looked back in resentment over her shoulder at the two women. "Oh! I have never—in my entire life—"

"Hold on to yourself," he interrupted, "until we get someplace we can't be seen." Jake suppressed a grin. He stopped before the ticket booth of the midway's rickety fun house, said something to the man in charge, dug into his jeans for a few bills, then took Toby by the hand and pulled her inside.

A blast of air rushed up from the floor as they stepped past the distorting mirrors and into the darkness. Toby was startled by the large, lighted plastic clown's head that suddenly thrust itself out of the blackness, gave a horrible parody of a laugh, then disappeared. The floor beneath their feet was unsteady and seemed to shift constantly, shaken by a motor beneath the boards.

Jake stopped, leaned against a wall in the darkness and wound his arm around Toby almost protectively. He began to laugh so hard that soon, she, too, was laughing. She giggled and buried her face against the starched cleanness of his shirt. He pressed his cheek against her hair and tried to stop laughing.

"Those women were awful!" he managed to say at last, and drew her closer.

"I thought Marietta might get you," Toby admitted, trying to get her breath. "And I'd have to ride home alone." She tried to look up at him in the darkness, but could see only the most shadowy outline. He was extraordinarily close to her, but that suddenly seemed quite right.

"Get me? Marietta? That mantrap? She's been a dangerous predator since she was eleven years old. Besides, who could take Mrs. Ekdahl for a mother-in-law? A man would be better off on Devil's Island."

"Teach her maid to make spaghetti," Toby said, scoffing at the memory.

"And Marietta just 'loves' to help the handicapped." He laughed. "Oh, God. And when she said that about you going back to 'your own kind' I nearly laughed in her face. The look in your eyes, Toby. You should have seen it—it should have knocked her flat." He rested his chin on the top of her head and laughed at the memory. Again she was surprised at how warm his laugh could be.

Companionably, she had put her arm around his waist. "Well," she challenged, "where did you get the nerve to tell that terrible lie that I'm an orphan? That's awful! I probably have a bigger family than anybody you've ever met— if you count all my aunts and uncles and cousins."

"I had to give her some reason why I was keeping you," he teased, then kissed her lightly, just beneath the ear.

Unbidden emotion flooded through her; passionate and, at the same time unwanted. She tried to draw away from him, but he held her fast. The situation, which a few seconds before had seemed cozy, was suddenly charged with risk. All morning she had watched him manipulate the emotions of others. Now he was turning his expertise to her.

"Don't," she said sharply. "You're not going to keep me. You want me gone. We both know it, so why lie about it?"

She wished fervently they weren't in the darkened fun house, and that the floor didn't continue to pitch beneath them, practically forcing her to keep clinging to him.

The arm that held her so closely tensed. In the near-blackness she could barely see him draw his head back.

There was an abrupt restraint in the way he touched her, yet the laughter stayed, cool and mocking, in his voice. "I told you, I have to fend off these dauntless huntresses. What better way—till I'm drawing again—than to pretend you've already caught me?"

At that moment, the plastic clown head appeared again, gave its jeering hoot of laughter, then disappeared into the darkness. The floor bucked harder than usual, throwing her more firmly into his embrace.

She struggled to keep her thoughts and desires from kidnapping her reason. This lightless place, where she had lost all sense of direction and where even the ground shifted uncertainly, made her want to cling to his warmth and strength as if it were survival itself. She wanted to remember the laughter they had shared, to glory in the perturbing thrill of his touch, to savor the words he had said outside, the gestures of affection he had shown her.

Except, she cautioned herself desperately, those words, those gestures had been lies, every last one. He used her as efficiently outside the studio as he did within it. He was perilously good at using her. And she was ripe for being used, for, foolishly, she wished all his silken, self-serving lies were true.

She took a step backward as best she could, but even though he allowed her to put that small distance between them, his arms still held her fast.

"Who plays this part next year?" she said between her teeth. "Will you have to hire a professional actress to keep all these poor, smitten women from mauling your irresistible self?"

His fingers tightened on her waist, hard enough to make her take in her breath sharply. "You're suddenly very cold, Moranti. What's wrong? I thought we were having fun."

"You're having fun," she corrected, trying to keep the tremor from her voice. "I just forgot for a moment that I'm only your decoy for the day. Now people are going to think I'm a lot more than just your assistant. I'm sure it's all very humorous to you, driving off the hordes of amorous women, but—"

His hand moved swiftly to her shoulder. He gave her a slight but hard shake. "I don't consider them amorous women," he returned, his voice hard. "I consider them hypocritical and avaricious women. Do you think Mrs. Ekdahl would ever have had me in her house when I was just the grandson of that hard-nosed, peculiar old preacher and didn't have a dime in my jeans? Do you think any of them even saw my brother or me when we were two skinny kids whose only friend was Cora and who were so shy we never did anything but hide out up in the attic and draw, hour after hour? No, Mona Lisa—I became prime husband material only when my bank account started looking a lot better than my past did. And there aren't hordes of women—just a few, like Mrs. Elofson and Mrs. Ekdahl. They want to use me, dammit, and I can laugh at them if I want. They deserve laughing at, because they're transparent as glass, the harpies."

His hand had released her shoulder, but slid back beneath her hair, to rest tantalizingly on her nape. "A moment ago you were laughing yourself," he said, his voice low.

The inside of the fun house was close as well as dark—almost airless—but Toby's nerves tickled icily at the intimate tenor of his voice, the electric caress of his hand against her sensitive skin. "You're—" she was unable to stop the tremble in her voice "—you're so hard to understand. It's like you're more than one person. You're one with me, and a different one with Cora, and another still with the children and people like Knut Hansen, and still somebody else with those women—"

"I'm the same person, Toby," he said. His fingers moved to her face, tracing the satiny line of her jaw. "It's not so hard to understand."

"It is," she said, struggling to breathe evenly. "Things you won't even discuss at home, like your—your recovery, you talk about it to other people as casually as the weather. But up on the hill we don't dare even mention it in front of you."

He paused in the darkness for a moment, then his forefinger moved to gently follow the curving line of her upper lip. "It's easier to talk to the people here," he said, in that same low voice. "They believe me when I say I'm going to be fine. You and Cora don't—do you?"

"I—" She turned her face from his touch, her emotions suddenly in sickening combat. "We...don't want you to be disappointed. Neither of us trust Hyde-Crippen. He makes us—frightened for you. And you're pushing yourself too hard."

There was a long moment of silence. The blackness seemed to press in on them. His forefinger found her lips again, pressed against them in the command to be silent.

"If you're frightened for me," he said at last, "then you must care for me. And if you care for me, Toby, you should believe in me."

His voice was beguiling, even seductive. His hand moved to the back of her neck again, tilting her face upward. She did not resist him when his lips descended to take hers. He kissed her with surprising gentleness, a tenderness that sent haunting tremors through her body.

Impulsively, almost hungrily, she put her hands to his face, feeling the masculine sculpture of his cheekbones beneath her sensitive fingertips.

"Toby," he said against her lips, and she realized that he was calling her by her first name, for no one's benefit but her own, and it sounded like poetry.

Then he kissed her again with an urgency that intoxicated her, sending a shock of yearning and desire through her. Her lips parted and he tasted deeply the moist silkiness of her mouth, and she his. She was no longer sure if the floor was shifting and moving beneath them in the darkness, or if Jake's touch, his kiss, had somehow made the earth itself quake.

"Toby," he said again in a harsh sigh. "I—" His breathing had gone ragged, and so, she realized dizzily, had hers. "I don't know how to tell you this," he said finally, drawing back from her briefly. Then swiftly, his mouth descended and he took one more brief but soul-shattering kiss. Once more he drew back, as if reluctantly, and she could feel him staring down at her through the darkness as if he were a cat.

"Tell me what?" she asked weakly.

He held her a moment longer, and she thought for one delicious moment he was going to kiss her again. Instead, she felt his hand leave her throat. She felt him swat her on the bottom with brotherly familiarity, and he laughed.

The change in tone jolted her. "I hate to tell you," he said, his voice cynical, "but our five minutes are up."

She tried to look up at him, but all she could see was blackness. She felt betrayed, mortally wounded. "What five minutes?" she asked, disbelief in her tone.

"The five minutes I bribed the ticket seller to let us have alone," he answered. "Come on. I thought we needed to get out of sight awhile. It was a pleasant break, even rather stimulating. Of course, I haven't had many thrills lately, so maybe I'm not a reliable judge. But it's a nice surprise—you do like me, don't you? In spite of yourself.''

There was such a note of bored superiority in his voice that anger flared through her. She pushed away from him, determined to escape. She was grateful for the darkness, for if she could see him, she was sure she would kill him.

"I don't like you," she said between her teeth. "I not only don't like you—I can't stand you. You're *impossible*!''

She tried to flee, but immediately was blocked by a wall—the fun house was not only dark, it was a maze. She wheeled and tried another direction, only to encounter another wall. Angry, disoriented, close to tears, she turned again, and felt his hand seize hers.

"Come on," he ordered. "You'll never get out of here by yourself. You don't have any sense of direction."

I certainly don't, she thought turbulently. *I don't have any sense at all. Why do I keep letting him do this to me—the smug bastard?*

Yet she had no choice but to let him keep her hand imprisoned in hers and to follow, haltingly, where he led. Somehow, he seemed to be able to see in the darkness when she could not, and somehow, he unerringly found a way where she could find none. He led, and she was helpless to do anything but follow.

CHAPTER EIGHT

JAKE'S HAND was still clamped tightly around hers as they finally emerged from the maddening confines of the fun house. She felt her face was flushed, her lips suspiciously naked and swollen by his kisses, and her heart hammered in confusion, resentment and hurt. People glanced at them surreptitiously and smiled, as if knowing exactly what the pair had been up to in the darkness.

He knew how to use everything to his advantage, she thought bitterly. She tried to draw her hand from his, but he refused to release it. He merely glanced down at the stiff, guarded expression on her face. "Stop looking so sulky," he ordered. "Look like you love being here. That's your job, remember."

"I don't love being here," she said with an emphatic toss of her head. "My job is to draw, not to pretend to make goo-goo eyes at you."

He gave her hand a squeeze that was neither gentle nor affectionate. "Don't be silly," he hissed. "You like me well enough, and we both know it. Under different circumstances, I might rather like you back."

The only sound Toby was capable of making was a small growl deep in her throat. He laughed. "I can't believe it," he said, shaking his head. "Your hair's already coming loose again. Let me help you pin it back."

"I can do it myself," she snapped, snatching her hand from his. She unfastened the clip, pulled her hair back more tightly and redid the fastening. "I really don't know what you want from me, Ulrick," she said, staring up at him in suspicious scrutiny.

"It's easy," he almost purred, taking her hand in his again. "First, I want you to draw 'Heartland' until I'm able to—which, believe it or not—is going to happen. Second, I ask you to go along with the harmless charade that I'm interested in you—just for today. It keeps women like Mrs. Ekdahl and their sacrificial maidens out of my hair."

"And that's all?" she asked skeptically.

He shrugged lackadaisically. "About all," he muttered. "That—and I'd like you to go to bed with me from time to time. You do have the damned most distracting profile in the world, you know—and a body that takes me back to the best days of anatomy class."

"What?" Toby demanded, her eyes flashing darkly. She looked around wildly. Children were milling in happy disorder in the midway, a barker hawked a game from a gaudy booth, and the air was filled with the scent of dust, cotton candy and frankfurters. A rickety ferris wheel creaked across the way. She could not think of a less likely place to be propositioned.

"What?" she repeated, half in rage, half in dismay.

Deftly he turned her so her back was to the side of a cotton-candy stand and his body shielded hers from the crowd.

"Oh," he mocked, raising one bronzed eyebrow, "I don't want anybody to see that face. Nobody will believe you love me."

"Love you?" Toby returned hotly, although she managed to hold her voice to a whisper. "I don't even like you. And for somebody trying to be romantic, you have a terrible sense of setting, a horrible sense of timing and the most colossal nerve since—since—"

Words failed her. He shook his head in weary toleration.

"You do so like me," he contradicted. "And, all right, I admit it, I like you. But I'm a comic strip artist and so are you. What better place to proposition you than outside the fun house and next to the tent with the fat lady? Besides, in case you haven't noticed, I'm not the romantic type.''

"That's not the problem,'' Toby said, putting her hand to a forehead that suddenly ached. ''The problem is you're not even the decent type. You're beyond my powers of description. And you have no right whatsoever to think I'd ever be your—your—''

"This is great fun,'' he said, looking bored, ''watching you cast around for a word your virtuous lips won't dare say. How about 'paramour'? How about 'temporary mistress'? How about 'lover'—that's nice and simple, and no longer implies commitment.''

"I told you,'' she said, pressing her fist to her brows and shaking her head. ''No. Don't even think of it.''

"I like to think of it,'' he mocked, ''and we could have a lot of fun in bed. What better way to end a long day's work? You're there. I'm there. We both need a way to get the tension out of our systems. We're both adults.''

A blessedly familiar voice cut into the conversation. ''What's wrong? Have you upset that girl?''

Toby looked up, blinking fast, and was relieved to see Cora standing there, eyeing the two of them critically. Cora looked very attractive, decked out in amber slacks, shirt and shoes. The tall lean man beside her had iron gray hair, and although he was not exactly handsome, his face had such simple honesty and humanity in it that Toby liked him immediately.

Jake flashed Cora and Herbert Olssen a sidelong smile. He greeted them easily, then said, ''Toby got a bit disoriented in the fun house. She'll be fine.''

"Is that so?'' Cora asked, cocking a dark eyebrow.

"Yes,'' Toby murmured. ''Really.'' She had no desire to let anyone ever know what Jake had just proposed.

"Hmmm,'' said Cora, still watching them both suspiciously. ''You look almost faint, Toby. Do you want an aspirin? Or to sit down?''

Toby shook her head and wrestled with emotions under control. "I'm fine," she insisted.

Cora didn't look convinced, but she chose not to pursue the subject. Instead, she introduced Toby to Herbert Olssen, who linked his arm gallantly through Cora's and nodded fondly at her. "Isn't this some lady?" he asked Toby proudly. "If she was any brighter, you'd have to wear sunglasses to look at her."

Smiling, Toby agreed. Cora herself smiled slightly, as if pleased but preoccupied. The older woman's black eyes were watching Jake now, very carefully, as if she were worried about him. "I'd like to talk to you a minute," she said, her eyes never leaving his. Her voice was abrupt. Then she glanced distractedly at Toby and Herbert Olssen. "If you two would excuse us a moment," she added, almost mechanically.

"You bet," Herbert said agreeably, smiling as he watched Cora lay a proprietory hand on Jake's arm and walk with him out of earshot. "She's somethin', isn't she?" Herbert said, never taking his eyes from Cora. "Queenly, that's how I always think of her. Spirited and queenly. Reminds me of my grandmother. Part Ponca Indian blood, my grandma—and beautiful when she was ninety years old."

Toby nodded. She was pleased that Cora had found not only an attractive but also a devoted suitor, yet she wondered what Cora was saying to Jake. The older woman's face was so intent, so serious, that Toby wondered if something was wrong. Yet Jake listened as if what she said was of no importance. He had his thumb hooked over his belt and was staring off into the distance as if bored.

"What do you suppose that's all about?" Toby asked Herbert, indicating the conversation from which they had been excluded.

"Couldn't say," he answered mildly. "But I have the feeling she saw somebody here who gave her a start. Don't know who. Maybe that doctor fellow. She thought he was gone for the day."

"Doctor?" Toby asked in surprise. She supposed Herbert meant Hyde-Crippen. She had hardly thought of the little man all day and had never wondered about his whereabouts. "Where's he supposed to be?" she queried.

"Couldn't say," Herbert repeated with the same mild calm. "Believe he told Cora he was going to Lincoln to do research in the medical library. But, mayhap, he's changed his mind. Cora surely doesn't like that man. Though I can't say why."

Cora was still talking, more passionately now, to Jake, who managed to look less interested than before. Toby tried to concentrate on Herbert Olssen instead. "Have you ever met Hyde-Crippen?" she asked.

"Yep," he said laconically.

"Well," Toby offered, feeling a bit defensive, "doesn't he strike you as the tiniest bit odd?"

"Odd as a man," Herbert answered casually. "I don't really know anything about him as a doctor."

"What's the difference?" she asked. "The man and the doctor are the same person."

"Now that," he said, casting her an amused hazel-eyed glance, "is where Cora and I differ. It's like a rabbit dog I had once. Most atrocious personality I have ever encountered in a canine. That dog was as obnoxious as a hive of hornets."

Toby looked at the lanky man with new interest. "Just what's that got to do with it?" She smiled, intrigued in spite of herself.

Herbert returned her smile with a knowing one of his own. "He just happened to be the best darn rabbit dog I ever saw. There's people like that, too, you know. It doesn't do to judge all of them by a part of them. 'Course, Cora isn't the easiest person in the world to convince, once she's got her mind made up. Nor," he added with a sly warmth, "are you, I'll warrant."

Toby flushed and traced the toe of her pink shoe in the dust. Herbert Olssen might give the impression of quiet indolence, but his observations were all too keen. No wonder he'd managed to hold Cora's interest these many years. She was spared trying to answer his gentle gibe by the return of Cora and Jake.

Herbert once again tucked Cora's hand though his arm and smiled benignly at her. Cora patted her hand absently, but her worried eyes were still on Jake. They darted a minute, their glance unreadable, to Toby, then back to Jake.

Jake seemed oblivious to the concern on Cora's face. "So," he said heartily, "we'll probably see each other again before it's over. Are you going to the community sing-along and church supper? Maybe we can eat together."

They parted, and Jake, in a gesture that was becoming all too disturbingly familiar, put his arm around Toby's waist. "What did Cora want?" she asked. "Why did she look so worried?"

"Nothing," Jake said shortly. He didn't bother to look down at her. He nodded in greeting to an elderly couple.

"Is Hyde-Crippen here?" she asked, searching desperately for even a semineutral subject.

"I don't know where he is," Jake answered idly. "I thought he went into the city. He probably wants go on a nice, complete bender and to hide from Cora—and you."

"Me?" she asked, taken aback. "Why me?"

"Because the poor man is taken with you," he answered, giving her a brief, satiric look. "Not that you should be too flattered. He's taken by most creatures capable of wearing skirts. But you're the one who's around most, so you're the one he has fantasies about. Another problem that would be solved, incidentally, if you'd sleep with me. Hyde-Crippen would let you alone. He knows which side his bread is buttered on."

"Stop talking like that," she snapped, glaring up at him. "I don't want to sleep with you. Never bring up the subject again."

"Moranti, my inhibited dear," he said, half laughing, "you may talk like the last virgin in twentieth-century America, but you kiss like a woman who not only wants to make love, but needs to. Why fight it?"

She looked up at him coldly. "Because," she said as frigidly as she could, "I have more sense than to get involved with you. You're my employer. I'm your employee. That's that."

He paused and stared down at her. Looking into his fervent blue gaze was like looking at a wall that shut out all knowledge of what lay behind.

"Maybe you're partially right," he said, his mouth curling slightly. "Maybe you are too smart to get involved with me. Maybe. Because you are smart, Moranti. You're very smart."

If I'm so smart, she thought, her knees beginning to tremble, *how can you still make me feel this way? If I'm so smart, why did I ever stay here so you can do this to me?*

As if he could read her thoughts, his smiled curved a little higher. "But I think you want me, Moranti. And you know it."

She looked up at him, tall and tawny-gold in the afternoon light, and summoned all her willpower to push back her unwanted emotions. He told her repeatedly how she felt about him. But he never said what he felt for her. And she knew why. Because he felt nothing. She was there. And he would find it amusing to make her need him in ways he would never need her.

She took a deep breath to steady herself. She hoped it also gave the effect that she was growing bored with the conversation. "As you once told me," she said, her voice as even as she could make it, "you have a very vivid imagination. So go on imagining whatever you want. And because the pay's so good, I'll pretend whatever you like—in public. For today. Though I doubt I'm a good enough actress to bring it off. We'll see."

As if to defy him and her own feelings, she stood on tiptoe and gave him the briefest of kisses on his chin. He looked down at her, an expression akin to surprise playing in his eyes.

"Do you think everyone saw that?" she challenged him. "Or should I do it again?"

"Do it again if you want," he answered, his eyebrow cocking cynically.

"No," she said brightly, settling in beside him and taking his arm. "I don't want."

He raised his eyebrow and smiled at nothing in particular. "Your problem, Mona Lisa," he drawled, "is that you haven't got the faintest idea what you want."

THE REST OF THE AFTERNOON PASSED in a blur of confusing images for Toby. She walked the midway with Jake, observing his interactions with the people of Zion Bluff. Although, as always, he kept part of himself closed off, she perceived real warmth and satisfaction in him today, a private man's carefully given love. Jake knew who he was and where he needed to be. He seemed to belong to this land the same way that the hills and rivers and trees did.

Well, Toby thought, trying hard to understand this puzzling and contradictory man, *this is why he's never left Zion Bluff. In spite of everything that's happened, this is home to him. He draws his strength from here.*

Jake constantly had to extricate himself and Toby from the attention of the children, who frequently tagged after him as if he were a Pied Piper. The more she watched him with them, the more she realized how well he understood them, and with what charm and imagination he bewitched them.

She knew there were a few people Jake did not like. They were the users: the women trying to win him in the marriage sweepstakes, the slick businessmen interested in Jake's money rather than in Jake. She saw that he handled them with great aplomb, a smiling politeness that no one was astute enough to realize was a parody of respect.

She wondered again which was the real Jake—this man of easy smiles and measured warmth for his neighbors—or the brooding, mercurial man who fought his private war up on the bluff, and drove Toby half mad with his contrariness.

When, late in the afternoon, he noticed she was tiring, he made her sit with him on a park bench by the band shell. Toby was exhausted from walking. She was also stuffed from tasting the entries in the chili contest, sampling the delicious free corn on the cob, and tasting the pies offered by the Ladies' Auxiliary.

She and Jake sat on the wrought iron bench and listened to a nattily groomed cowboy quartet harmonize favorite songs: "Don't Fence Me In," "I've Got Spurs" and "The Cowboy's Lament."

The park was lush and green, the music nostalgic, the ambience friendly, proud and innocent. Toby felt as if she had slipped through some sort of time warp. Despite the disquieting nearness of Jake, it seemed as if she had gone back to a purer, simpler and better time. This, she realized, was a real old-fashioned celebration, in a real old-fashioned hometown, among people who were for the most part genuine, idealistic and unpretentious.

She and Jake sat in silence until he again disconcerted her by seeming to read her thoughts. "People in the cities," he said, his voice meditative, "forget there still are places like this in America. Home places. These places are struggling to survive, you know." His finely boned face went suddenly serious. "In a hundred years there may be no more towns like Zion Bluff. The cities will draw away the young people. The conglomerates will finally beat the farmers.

And all this, and what it stood for, will be gone. That's one reason I stay—to record it.''

She turned to look at him. She was tired of her own conflicting thoughts and lulled by the simple, sincere emotion of the music. ''And the other reason you stay is that you love it, isn't it?'' The question was bold, more personal than he liked, but she had asked so softly, he took no offense.

''Some of us can't love any other kind of place.'' He nodded, still serious. ''A small town has its disadvantages, God knows. Everybody knows everybody else's business. Which cuts down nicely on pretension. As one of the best sages of the small town said, *Sumus quod sumus*.''

''What's that mean?'' she asked. Weary, she fought the desire to lean her head against his shoulder.

''It means, 'We are what we are.' No more, no less. It's sort of the Latin equivalent of 'What you see is what you get.'''

His intent blue eyes were locked searchingly with hers. ''So what do you see, Toby?'' he asked.

The question sent her hard-won equilibrium skittering off once more. ''I see a town,'' she said slowly. ''A little town—in what Cora called 'the heart of the heart of the country.'''

''And,'' he asked, his fingers toying provocatively with hers, ''what's your verdict on the heart of the heart of the country?''

''I like it,'' she said simply. ''I like it very much. It's almost like—coming home. Life where I come from is too crowded, too complicated, too fast. It's more natural here—scaled down to a size and a pace that the human mind can contend with.''

He looked down at their linked hands. ''And what about me?'' he asked, teasing. ''What do you see?'' His eyes met hers again and she felt her heart lurch at the impact of his gaze.

"I told you," she said stubbornly, feeling her body stiffen. "I don't know. What I like about this town, this area—is that it's not complicated. But you are. Too complicated."

He only smiled. He glanced at their linked hands again, then released her from his grasp. "Ah," he said with something between a sigh and a laugh, "you may be right."

"You said," she ventured, "that you had a brother. You said so in the fun house. Are you ever going to tell me about him?"

That familiar closed expression stole over his face. Then he looked into her eyes, and it was as if his guardedness flickered away. "I had a twin brother. He drowned. We were—close. I don't talk about him much. Maybe someday I'll talk about him to you."

An excited and irrational happiness stirred within her at the thought he might, at last, confide in her. "How soon is someday?" she asked softly.

"Just someday," he said evasively. "You know, Toby, maybe that's one reason I've been hard on you. You're the first person who's ever been inside 'Heartland' except for Raynor—my brother—and me. You're the only other person who's ever drawn any of those characters. After he died, I treated it like a sanctuary, I guess. You seemed like an invader, a usurper."

"Do I still?" she asked, her heart starting to beat with unwarranted hope.

He took her hand again, and gave her fingers a slight squeeze. He looked away from her, up into the wide blue sky. "I think you would have delighted him," he said. "You would have knocked him out. He'd say, 'She lives here, too, you jerk. Give her a break!'"

"I think I would have liked him," she said, studying Jake's face. But he seemed to be closing himself off again, as if he'd said too much. "Most people did like him," he said with unexpected terseness. "He was very likable. And those who knew Raynor well loved him."

"Including you?" she probed, for she sensed a darkness moving beneath the surface of the conversation, more secrets that swam like shadows in the depths of things.

"Especially me," he said curtly.

Toby felt the conversation had gone too far, and it was over.

An awkward yet significant silence rose like a wall between them. They were saved from it by the appearance of another group of children. This one was led by the bold little red-headed boy, who was clamoring for a story. Jake finally agreed—and the children sprawled on the grass around the bench, listening as Jake spun out a hoary and exaggerated tale of the great Nebraska folk hero, Febold Feboldson.

Toby smiled in spite of herself, for Jake was an excellent storyteller. The children begged for more, but Jake stood suddenly, his face almost a mask. "That's enough for a while, gang," he said. "We'll draw some more later." His voice, animated a moment before, was now preoccupied. Abruptly, he excused himself. He strode toward a stand of willow trees beyond the band shell.

The children, philosophical, picked themselves up off the grass and scattered. Toby, vaguely disturbed, hardly noticed them go. She watched Jake's tall figure. He was walking more slowly now, and he was moving toward someone who stood near the willows.

It was a woman. A very tall woman. And from where Toby sat she looked stunning. Toby had thought Marietta Ekdahl was lovely, but this woman made Marietta look ordinary, almost plain.

She stood alone by the swaying willows, and her body seemed to radiate drama the way the sun gives off light. She wore a flowing, unbelted black creation, which the breeze made play intriguingly against her slender body. The dress had a deeply scooped neck and was printed boldly with a large white flower on one breast, and a modernistic border of larger flowers at the hem. It was the kind of dress that made its wearer center stage, no matter where she stood.

A wide-brimmed white hat shadowed her brow, yet could not disguise the delicate and fine-boned features of her face. In spite of the theatrical sumptuousness of the woman's pose and attire, what Toby noticed most was her hair. Impossibly thick, silvery blond, it cascaded loosely to her shoulders in luxuriant and studied disorder.

Denise, Toby thought with a shaft of jealous insight that was almost clairvoyant in intensity. Denise, the long-lost fiancée. That was who Cora had seen. She was back. She was also alone. She might have married someone else, but from the way she watched Jake's approach, her husband was not on her mind. Nobody was, except the tall blond man who moved with slow purposefulness toward her.

Toby took a deep breath. From the way the tall woman waited, and from the fateful way Jake moved toward her, it seemed they must feel the world held only the two of them. Toby felt suddenly useless, unneeded and unwanted. She also felt slightly ridiculous. She was, after all, only an ordinary young woman in blue jeans and a plain pink sweater and dusty pink canvas shoes. Her hair was coming loose in unruly tendrils, she wore no makeup, and she knew, from the morning's ride that she probably smelled faintly of horse.

Jake had been using her for a decoy all day, and perhaps this rendezvous with the tall woman by the willow tree was the real reason. Denise, after all, was married—or at least had been. What better way to throw dust into the eyes of a curious small town than to pretend interest in someone totally unlike Denise? *Used again,* Toby thought bitterly.

Feeling sick with disappointment, she rose from the bench and made her way hastily back toward the midway. At the edge of the park she almost bumped into Herbert and Cora.

Herbert was carrying a pair of pink teddy bears he had won in the shooting booth for Cora, and both he and she were decked with leis he had won at the baseball toss. But Cora's face told Toby that she, too, had seen what was taking place by the willows.

Herbert looked at Cora's unhappy expression and Toby's stricken one without comprehension. Then he followed Cora's black, burning gaze and saw Jake and Denise standing by the trailing fall of the willow boughs.

Neither Jake nor Denise spoke. They only stood, she staring up at him, he looking down at her. Her only movement was to take off the broad-brimmed white hat so that the gentle summer breeze blew through the unconfined wealth of her shining hair.

"Uh-oh," Herbert said, in the voice of a man who suddenly realizes he is in the midst of a complex situation. "Who's that?" His eyes were fixed on the blond in the compelling black dress.

"That," Cora muttered between her teeth, "is trouble. That's what that is."

"Denise?" asked Toby. Her voice sounded like a powerless squeak in her ears.

"Denise," confirmed Cora, her tone disgusted.

"Oh," Herbert said, looking depressed. "*That* Denise. She's blonder."

"Denise," Cora said with ill-disguised dislike, "is the sort of woman who will always be blonder."

Across the park, they saw Denise lift a slender hand adorned with black and silver bangles. Softly she touched Jake's cheek. Her fingers lingered, not moving away.

Slowly Jake lifted his own hand and pushed Denise's beautiful, abundant hair back from her face. He held it back a moment, the better to see her delicate features. The gesture actually made Toby's heart hurt—he had done nearly the same thing to her so many times.

"I thought she upped and married somebody else years ago," muttered Herbert. "So why's she looking up at him like that?"

"They were engaged—remember?" Cora said shortly. "Until she threw him over for that doctor twice her age. I don't think she ever got Jake out of her system, though. Or that he got over her."

"Oh," Herbert said noncommittally, then cleared his throat in embarrassment.

"I should have known," Cora muttered. "I should have known—things always go wrong all at once. First the accident, now this. I wondered about those letters coming from Baltimore all of a sudden. I wondered about the phone ringing in the middle of the night. Sometimes it'd come on me like a cold chill. I'd think—she's got tired of that doctor, and she's coming back for Jake. So this is why he wanders around all hours of the night. In addition to everything else, he's got *her* on the brain again."

"Now, Cora—" Herbert began, patting her arm. "You don't know for sure—"

"What else is she doing in a town like this?" Cora demanded stubbornly, darting a challenging look up at him. "And look at the way she's staring at him—like she'd eat him up with her eyes."

Toby turned her back on the scene so she wouldn't have to see how true Cora's words were.

"Say," Herbert said with sudden heartiness, "it's almost time for the community sing and the dinner social to begin. What say we get over to the church grounds and get us a good seat, eh, girls?"

"Sure," Toby said with artificial brightness, putting her hands in the hip pockets of her jeans. She wanted to leave the scene—the haunting picture of the two handsome people silhouetted against the willows—behind her.

"Why not?" Cora said crisply. "And if he wants to find us, let him figure out where. But if he brings her around after all she did—"

"Cora—" Herbert said, his tone fond but warning.

"Oh, I know!" Cora answered in despair, shaking her head. "It's just—so much seems to be happening this summer, and none of it good, Herb."

"I know, I know," he said gently. He took her arm, then gallantly offered Toby his other. She took it gratefully. But she couldn't help throwing one last glance over her shoulder as Herbert escorted them down Maple Street and toward the church.

But now the willows swayed rhythmically, alone with the wind. Jake and the beautiful woman in black were gone. Toby felt more alone than she'd ever felt in her life.

CHAPTER NINE

TOBY TOYED listlessly with her silverware. She sat with Herbert and Cora at one of the many card tables set on the church lawn. White tablecloths fluttered in the breeze, genial chatter filled the late afternoon air, sparrows twittered in the maple trees. The community choir, resplendent in white shirts and blouses, sang from the steps of the church. It was an archetypal picture of small-town conviviality, but Toby felt solitary, locked in her own unhappy world.

Cora was laboring hard to talk herself into a better mood. "If he wants to make a mess of his life, he's certainly old enough," she grumbled. "It's none of my affair. Why should I worry?"

"That's right," Herbert agreed with more sympathy than sincerity.

"It's a free country," Cora continued. "He can pick up with anybody he wants. It's certainly no concern of mine." Her voice lacked assurance, as did most of Herbert's consolations.

With a start, Toby felt a familiar hand on her shoulder. All her muscles tensed. She saw Cora and Herbert's eyes raise to Jake, who stood behind her.

"Go ahead and eat without me," he joked. "And steal my woman while you're at it." He gave Toby's hair a playful tug, then pulled out the remaining chair and sat down.

"We would have waited," Cora said pointedly, "but you seemed otherwise engaged."

"Denise? Well, you knew she was here," Jake said easily. "You saw her first. How's a man get something to eat around here?"

"Here," Toby said, tonelessly, handing him her untouched plate. "I'm not hungry."

"Thanks," he said, hardly glancing at her. "I'm starved. Cora, get that look off your face. I had to speak to Denise—she's just passing through on her way to see her grandmother in Yankton."

"Oh?" Cora said innocently. "Seems she's been just passing through for about an hour and a half. Where's her husband? Or did she just pass through her marriage, too?"

He gave the older woman one of his sardonic blue looks, and smiled slightly. "She claims he's about to be her ex-husband. He's still in Baltimore. She says it's been over between them for some time."

"Ha," snorted Cora, throwing her napkin on the table. "I thought so. Those letters from Baltimore with no return address, those phone calls late at night—"

"Shouldn't look at the postmarks on my private mail," Jake replied calmly, picking up a piece of chicken. "Shouldn't concern yourself about my personal phone calls." He bit into the chicken with the air of a man totally satisfied with himself.

"I don't care a bit about your old mail or your old phone calls," Cora said stubbornly, crossing her arms across her ample bosom. "I was just telling Herbert I certainly don't care what you do about that woman. Wasn't I?"

Herbert nodded. "She was telling me and telling me," he said.

"Good," Jake replied. "Fine. Then you won't mind if she comes and stays with us."

Toby struggled not to flinch. She bit the inside of her lip, very hard. Why are you feeling so sorry for yourself, you little fool? she scolded herself. Cora warned you about Denise long ago. You knew he never cared anything for you.

"I won't mind *what*?" Cora asked with deadly quiet.

Jake bit into a homemade roll. His reply was blithe. "I said, 'you won't mind if she comes to stay with us.' In fact, I know you'll be a paragon of politeness and friendliness—won't she Herbert?"

"Oh, I suppose she will." Herbert sighed. "Even if it kills her."

"I can be polite to anybody I have to be polite to," Cora said defensively. "I can be polite with a vengeance."

"Um-hm," Jake said coolly. "It's the vengeance part I worry about."

"Me, too," Herbert said gloomily. He reached over and gave Cora's shoulder a pat. "Come on, Miss Whitewater, I think we need to take a little walk."

"Oh, Herbert," Cora said impatiently.

"Cora," Herbert repeated. "A walk, Cora."

"Oh, all right," she agreed unhappily. "Thank heaven there's one sane man around here."

Herbert rose, held Cora's chair for her and then escorted her with great courtliness back toward the park.

"Ah, Herbert's a gem," Jake said, attacking his potato salad. "Whenever Cora gets in one of her snits, he can walk and talk her out of it. It's a good thing he likes to walk. I'd say Cora put about five thousand miles on the poor man. But he adores her."

"She's very lucky," Toby said pensively.

He turned slightly and studied her. "And what's your problem, Mona Lisa? You look as funereal as Cora looks miffed. Don't tell me you're jealous—that would be more than my fragile ego could take."

"Your ego is about as fragile as Mount Rushmore," Toby returned with more spirit than she intended. "And I'm certainly not jealous. Why on earth would I be jealous?"

"No reason." He shrugged. "But I can dream, can't I?"

"I think," she said coldly, "that when you finish stuffing yourself, I'd like to go home."

"Fine," he replied, as if nothing were more agreeable. "I was going to go back anyway. I want to get Tango home before dark. And you really are being snippy. I'm not stuffing myself. I'm eating as daintily as a bird."

"A giant condor," Toby said uncharitably.

"Ha!" he laughed. "You are jealous. You listen too much to Cora, that's your problem. You've been that way from the start. Now you're upset about Denise. Serves you right for listening to idle gossip."

"I am not jealous," Toby insisted. "I don't care one bit."

"Not one bit?" he taunted. She tried to look as if she cared more about the ants that crawled through the grass. He slanted her a look she tried to ignore, then he finished his meal in silence. "Come on," he said, with an impatient sigh. "Let's go back to the house."

"Fine," she said shortly. She had no desire whatsoever to get back on that excitable horse with its flaring nostrils and wild eyes, but she fervently wanted to get to the house and be alone—as far from Jake as possible.

When they reached the rail fence bordering the park, Tango was stamping and tossing his head. Toby groaned inwardly. The horse was too like its master—too powerful and too unpredictable.

As Jake undid the reins from the railing, Toby found they were once again being surrounded by a small group of children.

"You're not takin' him home?" wailed the little red-headed boy. "Aren't you gonna have him do his tricks?"

"You always show his tricks!" accused a little girl who had a surprising mastery of the whine for one so young.

A chorus of voices chattered about them, and Toby had the feeling she and Jake were knee-deep in a group of small tired savages, some of whom were about to throw tantrums.

"Maybe I'll let him show off just a little," Jake conceded at last, giving Toby a wry look. "He's restless and wants to.

I can feel it pulsing through him. Mind waiting a few minutes?''

"Of course not." But she watched with concern as Jake borrowed a large kerchief from the red-headed boy. The child had obviously won the kerchief on the midway. It was black and printed with a pirate's skull and crossbones. Jake used it to bind his black-gloved injured hand to his belt.

"What are you doing?" she asked with alarm.

"Tango's 'tricks' get a bit on the rough side," he explained, frowning. "Help me with this knot, will you?"

She knew he hated asking for help. She went to his side quickly, and knotted the kerchief as firmly as she could. "Are you sure you should do this?" she asked nervously.

"Ah, we do it every year—but at the rodeo," he said. "I just never did it left-handed before."

Toby didn't like the sound of trick riding at all. A host of worries began to churn within her. "Jake—" she began, but he had already vaulted to Tango's bare back.

She could see the determination and the concentration on his face, and it frightened her.

"Everybody back," he ordered. "Way back. Because when I give this horse the signal, he's going to buck like crazy. If I see anybody closer to me than twenty feet, I stop. Understand?"

The children nodded, as did many of the adults beginning to gather. But as they obediently stepped back, Toby didn't move. She stared up at Jake, her face white and her eyes wide. *Buck? That was that wild-eyed horse's trick—it bucked?* She took three quick steps nearer, and she seized hold of the horse's bridle as she had seen Cora do. "No," she said simply and with force.

Jake tossed her a disbelieving grin, then nodded for her to let go. "No," she said again, her voice trembling. "Not bucking. Please. Please, Jake."

"Don't be silly," he said, stirring restlessly on the big animal's back. "Let go, Toby. I know what I'm doing." He stared down at her with a strange mixture of displeasure and amusement.

"It isn't worth it," she insisted desperately. She kept a tight hold of Tango's bridle with one hand, and the other, without thinking, she put on Jake's thigh in entreaty. "You could be hurt again. Don't take the chance. Please."

"Move, Toby," he ordered, but his eyes, locked on hers, held a strange expression.

"No," she repeated. "That's how this whole mess started. You can't."

"That was different," he scoffed. "I wasn't expecting it— and he fell. I'm fine. Stand back."

"No," she said, tilting her chin up. "If you want this crazy thing to buck, it can buck with me hanging onto it. If you want to kill yourself, you might as well take me with you. Because I'm not letting go."

She locked her fingers more tightly around the bridle.

Jake leaned over, resting his arms on Tango's silvery neck. He looked as casual as if he were sitting at a desk. He stared at her until she felt distinctly uncomfortable.

"I'll be damned," he said at last. "You mean it, don't you?"

She nodded, her heart beating fast.

"I don't believe this." He turned his face to the sky and gave a short bark of laughter. "I never saw such determination to spoil a man's fun. And you always tell me I'm impossible."

She said nothing. She only stood her ground.

"Kiss me and say please again," he ordered. "Maybe I'll cooperate. Come here."

She stood on her tiptoes, straining up toward him. He dipped his head and gave her a short, yet possessive kiss. Her heart, which had been beating far too fast, almost stopped. She dimly heard laughter and cheers from the crowd.

He broke off the kiss only to take another, shorter, yet more intense. All too briefly his lips burned against hers.

"Now," he said, his smile wicked, "tell me you do care. Tell me you're crazy about me. Too crazy to let me take a chance of getting hurt."

She stared up at him in frustration. He nodded. "Say it," he commanded.

She felt desperate and trapped. She took a deep breath. "All right," she said. "I care for you. Too much to let you take this kind of chance. Please don't do it."

"Ahh," he said. "Music to my ears." He looked at the crowd and made a gesture of amused helplessness. "Sorry," he said. "Just can't hurt the lady's feelings. Some of you boys may not understand now, but you will someday—believe me."

Part of the crowd laughed, part made a sound of disappointment. Toby stepped back slightly, blushing. Jake gave a parody of a sigh, reached down and untied the bandanna from his arm. He tossed it back to the red-headed boy.

"Besides," Jake said with his crooked smile, "I probably wouldn't be setting you kids a very good example. Next year I'll give you a show you won't forget. Till then—I want to keep the pretty lady happy."

He gave Toby another long look, then stretched out his hand to her. "Come on, Mona Lisa," he said. "Let's go home."

Still stunned that he had agreed to her wishes at all, she nodded. Wordlessly, she took his proffered hand and let him pull her up behind him. He turned, put his lips against her ear and whispered, "Killjoy."

Some people in the crowd, thinking he had uttered an endearment, tittered. Toby blushed harder.

"Hang on," Jake ordered, turning from her. Reluctantly she locked her arms around his waist. She glanced at the dispersing crowd. Then, suddenly, she understood why Jake had done as he'd done.

Standing alone at the rear of the crowd, her beautiful hair falling around her face, Denise watched them. She was extraordinarily pale, and her perfect features looked stricken.

Her eyes met Toby's for a split second. Her look was both wounded and defiant. *So,* she seemed to be saying, watching Toby with her arms around Jake, *so you're the enemy. You're the one he'll use to hurt me.*

Denise had seen it all, Toby realized as Tango sprang away. Indeed, Jake's whole change of heart must have been staged for Denise's benefit. Denise had been foolish enough to leave Jake. He was going to make her pay dearly before she got him back.

Toby felt used and slightly soiled. She was tired of Jake's games and vendettas. She wished she didn't have to hang onto him so tightly. Yet all day, he had contrived ways so that she had to do precisely that: cling to him. How he must enjoy it, she thought bitterly, remembering the expression on Denise's face.

"Well, Mona Lisa," he said, laughing, "I hope you're satisfied. But I couldn't have got hurt. I know every move Tango's going to make. I'm in complete control. But I was struck by a sudden and irrational desire to keep you happy— so I hope you are."

She stared at his back dumbstruck. Her hands, locked around his waist, seemed to freeze. Her eyes widened as she comprehended the enormity of that particular lie.

"Besides," he said, tossing her a smug glance over his shoulder, "I finally got you to say you cared. You really were frightened, weren't you? I'm touched."

Tango's trot grew brisker, and she had to hug Jake more tightly lest she be thrown. "Don't flatter yourself," she said harshly. "If you're dead, you can't authorize my paycheck, that's all."

"That's not what those big, dark, frightened eyes were saying," he taunted. "Good grief, I thought you'd be delighted you scored such an easy victory over me."

She knew his capitulation had been simply to make Denise temporarily jealous. "Letting this silly horse buck would be the stupidest trick you could pull," she said coldly. "You could have killed yourself."

"Could not have," he said, not bothering to glance at her. "I've been doing it since I was twelve years old. My brother and I flirted for a while with becoming rodeo riders instead of cartoonists. We used to go out to Herbert's farm and practice falling off his horse Bessie. And his cows. And out of his hayloft."

"I suppose that's how you hurt your arm," she accused, "showing off—being the big daredevil."

"I wasn't doing anything," he said evenly. "The snake struck at Tango. He reared and fell backward. It was nobody's fault. It was an accident."

"Anybody with a grain of sense should stay off this wild-eyed thing," she retorted.

"Life," he said, biting off his words, "is too short to go around being scared of things."

"So I suppose you'll really be letting him buck again? You would have done it back there," she accused.

He quickened Tango's pace, making her clutch his waist more tightly.

"I intend to do everything again," he shot back. "How often do I have to tell you? And don't criticise me for taking chances when you're scared to death of doing exactly that. It's hypocritical."

He kicked the horse into a canter, forcing Toby to hold him with all her strength. The warm air rushed past them, and Tango's hooves rumbled softly on the black earth of the road.

What did he mean, she wondered, hanging onto him furiously, that she was afraid to take chances? Was it simply another taunt intended to bring her to his bed? He had exploited her enough without that, she thought unhappily.

GRATEFULLY SHE ENTERED the house. Without saying another word to Jake, she strode purposefully upstairs. She kicked off her shoes, stripped off her dusty jeans and pink sweater, dropped her underwear in a lacy heap beside the bed, and took refuge in the cool spray of the shower. She wished she could wash the whole day from her mind and body.

Afterward, she dressed in her green shorts and halter. She pulled her damp hair back, but when she found herself pinning it with the malachite clip, she almost swore. He had her trying to please him out of habit now. It angered her, but she pinned the hair back anyway, just so it wouldn't spill down the way Denise's had. Not, she thought, bitterly, that there was any chance anyone would ever confuse her with the likes of Denise.

She got out her drawing pad and pencils and flopped miserably on the bed, piling the pillows behind her. She opened her drawing pad and stared at her latest attempts at "Taffy." They suddenly looked terrible to her—stiff, stupid, uninspired. She resisted the childish desire to rip out the page, crumple it up and fling it into the waste basket.

She turned instead to a clean page, took up her ruler, and began to divide the page into panels.

She was startled when a loud knock issued from her door. She knew Cora wasn't back; she doubted if Hyde-Crippen had returned. It must be Jake.

He pounded on the door again, hard. He called her name.

She drew her knees up higher beneath the drawing pad, scowled at the door and said, "Go away. I've seen enough of you for one day."

"What do you mean, go away?" he demanded. "We've got to get back to town. Are you decent?"

"I'm perfectly decent," she retorted, "which is why I want to keep a distance from you. I'm not going anywhere. I'll see you in the studio Monday. Now go away."

"Toby!" he warned.

She listened warily, wondering if she should get up and bolt the door. Then it was too late. He had swung it open, and stood in the doorway. He, too, had showered, and his hair gleamed in the lamplight. He wore a fresh white shirt, hip-hugging dark jeans, and black snakeskin boots.

"Go away," she repeated petulantly, but her heart seemed to start careening around wildly inside her chest. He stood there, looking at her in the center of the huge bed.

"What's wrong with you?" he asked, his hand still on the knob. "What are you doing? Why are you dressed like that?"

"I told you," she said, trying to look braver than she felt. "I'm staying here. I happen to have work of my own to do. I do have a life other than you, you know."

He looked at her, a speculative frown on his face. "You can't stay. We've got to go back. I promised those kids more pictures. What are you doing anyway? What are you drawing?"

She closed the drawing pad protectively, as if it exposed some part of her. "Nothing," she muttered.

"Don't be infantile," he said, coming toward her. He sat down beside her on the bed. She realized they were alone in the house, that he was in her bedroom, actually on her bed, and the thought made her feel ticklish and strange. He held out his hand for the drawing pad. "Show me."

"No," she said stubbornly. She refused to look at him.

"Oh, come on," he ordered firmly. The tone in his voice was almost kind. He reached over and took the pad from her. "Don't even bother to look," she said unhappily. She shifted to the edge of the bed, as far from him as she could get. "It's no good and that's exactly what you'll say—it's terrible. It's worthless."

She stared out through the opened drapes at the twilit bluffs and the first distant stars winking over the river. She heard him open the drawing pad, turn the pages.

"Do you want to explain this?" he asked at last, after a long and strained silence.

"There's nothing to explain," she said tonelessly. "It's a strip I made up in high school. It's called 'Taffy.' It's been rejected by everybody in publishing, so you don't have to tell me how bad it is. I know."

There was another beat of silence. For an irrational second she had the mad hope he would tell her that her work was good. He didn't.

"You're right," he said quietly. "It's terrible. It's worse than worthless. I can't believe you did it."

She had known he would say that, but still she felt as if she had been hit, and hard. She refused to flinch. He had hurt her so often today that once more should make no difference. She sat still as stone and kept staring out at the fading light.

"Satisfied?" she asked bitterly. "Now you have one more thing to feel superior about?"

"Don't be ridiculous," he scoffed. "I'm not satisfied. I'm astounded. Why are you wasting your time on garbage like this? 'Taffy.'" He said the last word with unmitigated scorn.

"I didn't think it was quite that bad," she said coldly. It took all her willpower to keep him from seeing how deeply his criticism slashed.

"From you, it is," he replied. "Good Lord—the drawing's wooden—these characters look like zombies. The jokes have no punch, and the whole idea's stale. It's been done a thousand times."

"All right," she said, wheeling to face him, "is there anything else you want to say? I didn't ask for your criticism, but go ahead—rip me completely to shreds. You're good at it, and you obviously enjoy it."

His blue gaze fairly crackled. "What I'm saying is that you're too good for this derivative junk, Toby. Why aren't you challenging yourself? Why aren't you using your talent?"

She raised her chin defiantly. "Because I have no talent," she shot back. "Because I can't create, I can only copy. I have no originality. I just follow what others do. I'm a hack—a lackey. I was born to be a lackey, and that's all I'll ever be."

"If you believe that," he said angrily, tossing the drawing pad to the floor, "you don't deserve to have talent. You ought to give it to somebody who appreciates it and take up scrubbing floors—if that's how you see yourself, as the poor slave."

Frustrated beyond tolerance she took her pencil and broke it in two with a sharp crack. "Will you please leave?" she asked, her voice small and shaking.

"No," he snapped. He reached over, took the broken pencil halves from her hands and threw them on the floor beside the drawing pad. "What's the matter with you? You're as spooky as a filly in her first lightning storm. You know the truth about that 'Taffy' trash—you knew it before I ever came through that door. And don't go feeling sorry for yourself, because you're not the type."

"If you won't go, I will," she said. She started to rise from the bed, but he seized her by the wrist and pulled her back. He put sufficient force into the motion that she fell to her back among the pillows. Without releasing his grip, he drew closer and bent over her.

"Will you just leave me alone?" she asked, looking up at him with apprehension and unhappiness. This time she couldn't keep the tears from welling in her brown eyes.

"Toby," he said severely, "don't cry. You're not that type, either. What I'm telling you is to use your potential— that's all. You've got a rare gift—exceptional talent—don't deny it. You've got intelligence. And passion. Great passion, I think. You don't even suspect how much."

She shut her eyes so she wouldn't have to look up at that handsome, harshly controlled face. She felt the hot tears

squeeze out between her closed lids, and she hated herself
for showing him weakness.

"Toby," he said, his voice low with fervent emotion,
"what's wrong? I'm not saying these things to hurt you. I
want to help you—any way I can. I know I'm hard on you,
or I seem to be, but I want the best for you. I want the best
of you—body and soul."

She couldn't answer him. She only stayed silent, feeling
the tears flow slowly down her cheeks.

"Don't," he said softly. He released her wrist, and gently
he wiped the tears away. "Don't be unhappy. I realized
when I saw you standing there holding Tango's bridle that
I hate seeing you unhappy. And I've come to realize that you
and Cora might be right. Maybe I won't have such a mirac-
ulous recovery after all. So until somehow I can draw again,
I need you."

"You don't need anybody," she said, then put her hand
across her mouth so he wouldn't see how her lips were beginning to tremble. "Least of all me."

"I need you," he breathed. His touch was surprisingly
tender as he pushed her fingers away and laid his own
against her lips. "I'm going to need you longer than I
wanted to admit—six months, nine months, maybe a year.
You could come to Hawaii with me. And when you finally
do leave—why can't we part on good terms? Friends. Why
not even lovers? Because I'm tired of fighting it, Toby. I
want you. I have from the start."

She opened her eyes to let her gaze lock combatively with
his. "How could we be lovers?" she challenged bitterly,
"when I don't love you, and you don't love me?"

He shrugged, his face impassive. He ran his forefinger
down the curve of her cheekbone. "It's just a word," he
said gruffly.

"Not to me it isn't," she said, turning her face so she
wouldn't have to experience the soft torture of his touch.
"You already have a stable of horses. I don't want to be part

of your stable of women. How many do you think you need, anyway?''

"One," he said, cupping her chin and turning her face back to his own. "Just one. At a time, that is."

He began to lower his mouth to hers, and Toby found her lips parting in helpless yearning. But his words pierced her consciousness like so many tiny poisoned darts, injecting a deadly cold into her.

He needed only one woman at a time. Toby this morning. Denise this afternoon. Toby tonight. Denise tomorrow. She knew what Jake wanted in this bed from her—power. Power over her. Over Denise. A way to give Denise a taste of her own medicine. To reduce her to a supplicant, the way he was trying now with Toby.

His lips were so close to hers, she could feel their warmth, making her own tingle.

"It's too bad you're not still a twin," she said acidly, striking out to protect herself from him however she could. "Think of all the women you could use then. How sad for the female sex that now there's only one of you."

He drew back from her abruptly. He stared down at her a moment, his eyes hard as blue ice. His sensuous mouth twisted into an ugly line. His hand had leaped from its gentle touch upon her face and now gripped the pillow, dangerously hard.

"That's the rottenest thing anybody's ever said to me," he said, his voice deadly quiet. "I didn't think you had it in you to be a bitch, Moranti."

His use of her surname jarred, but she felt it also set a wall of protection between them. "That's because you don't know much about people," she said with carefully controlled malice. "Except how to use them. And what's really impressive—" she raised herself slightly and looked pointedly at his injured hand in its black glove "—is you can still do it, so to speak, with one hand tied behind your back.''

He sat up, stared at her for an uncomfortable moment, then stood. "Why don't you put a little of that venom into your strip?" he demanded, smiling frostily. "Maybe it wouldn't be so boring."

Toby sat up and scurried off the other side of the bed. She stood, breathing hard as she stared back at him. "And why don't you go back to town and see if somebody else falls for your tough-guy, free-spirit, wham-bam-thank-you-ma'am style? I don't like it. But I'm sure others do."

"Yes," he said stonily. "Others do. Some of them. I could go to one now. But I wanted to be with you. Maybe I was a fool. It wouldn't be the first time."

Her fine nostrils flared and she glowered at him across the bed. Of course, she thought. Denise was waiting for him somewhere in town, or more probably outside, where nobody could witness the rendezvous. He would have toyed with Toby, taken her back to town, used her presence as a smoke screen once more, then left her to slip off to his tryst with Denise.

"So," he said, smiling faintly. He adjusted the black glove. "I'll see you at work. And don't take what I said about your strip the wrong way. You do have talent, you know. What you don't have yet is courage. You're afraid to take chances. And you're afraid to be honest. In your drawing and your life."

She said nothing, only glared at him harder. He kept that same maddening half smile, then turned and left the room. He closed the door behind him, carefully, without slamming it. Its click echoed with a soft finality.

Toby, spent, fell back to the bed and buried her face in the pillows. She fought not to cry, but she was emotionally exhausted. She was filled with longing, anger, confusion and shame.

The whole day seemed to spin crazily through her mind, like a film being run at insane speed. She regretted it all. Why, to cap everything, had she let him see the drawings of

'Taffy'? She'd known all along what he would say about her work. Worse, she knew what he said was true.

But more than that, she hated the humiliation of wanting, in spite of everything, to be in his arms, to feel his length pressed against her, his warm mouth taking hers. She loved him, she realized, although it went against all reason. And more than anything she wanted in her life, she wanted him to love her in return.

But she knew he never would. She was nothing to him but an instrument to control, a vessel that would satisfy occasional lust, a device to bring the beautiful Denise more completely under his domination—that was all.

Yet, ironically, what shamed her most of all was the cruelty of the words she had hurled at him. She had been vicious to him in order to protect herself. At that thought she did cry. What kind of stupid business was love, anyway, if it made you strike out at the very person you desired most?

She remained sleepless most of the night. She heard Cora and Herbert come in at about midnight, and Herbert leave shortly after. At three, she heard the familiar wheeze of Hyde-Crippen's car as he pulled into the drive of the guest house. She could have sworn she heard him trip over a bench on the lawn and fall. He was probably drunk.

It was almost six o'clock in the morning when she heard Jake's car in the drive. The sun was well up into the sky. He must have spent the night with Denise, who had never reached Yankton or her grandmother. And with all the insolence in the world, he was whistling.

CHAPTER TEN

THE ATMOSPHERE IN THE HOUSE was so tense the next morning that Toby had to escape. She dressed in her best white linen suit, borrowed a road map from Cora, got into the Mustang and fled.

She made the two-hour drive into Omaha and gratefully lost herself in the anonymity of the city. Again she was surprised at the sheer amount of space Omaha covered. It stretched along the meandering river hills, seemingly as limitless as the immense sky above.

She spent a good part of the day in the Joslyn Art Museum. It was a massive, yet graceful building of pink marble, set high on a hill in downtown Omaha.

But the beautiful displays of Western art did little to pacify her spirit. Cases showed the handicrafts of the Native Americans who had first looked on these vast regions, and though she admired the artistry of the pieces, they made her only think of Cora.

There were rare and marvelous paintings by the first explorer-artists who had recorded the wonders of the area. But the scenes of the now-familiar hills reminded her of Zion Bluff. So did the oils and sketches that portrayed the river—for the Missouri seemed to hold a particular fascination for those early artists. She thought of its bluffs and mighty currents. And she thought of Jake.

She tried to take solace in the beauty of the building's indoor floral court with its fountain and palms. But even in that almost oriental opulence, her thoughts were drawn back to the house on the bluffs. And to Jake.

An art museum, she decided at last, was not the place to forget about an artist. She took refuge in a movie theater and watched the same film three times.

She didn't get back to Zion Bluff until two in the morning. On her way to her room, she woke Cora, who had been sleeping restlessly in a rocker in the living room.

"Where have you been?" Cora demanded, sitting up straight and smoothing her long braids. "This whole house has gone crazy. I was afraid you'd run off. Clear back to New Jersey. I was worried about you. And Hyde-Crippen's gone, too."

"Hyde-Crippen?" Toby repeated, frowning in puzzlement. "And he's still not home?"

"I think he's on another toot." Great weariness showed on Cora's face. "I don't blame him. He took the cast off Jake's arm today. I think he knows he can't fool anybody any longer. There's still no feeling in that hand. And no movement. Not a bit. He's failed, Toby. Jake's no better at all."

Toby could say nothing. Numbly, she shook her head. She and Cora had both expected as much from the beginning. Hyde-Crippen had provided no miracles. Still, the failure, expected as it was, made her slightly sick. If Jake drew again at all, he would have to start from the beginning like a child, learning to use his left hand.

"Does Jake know?" she asked at last.

"He suspects," Cora replied, sighing. "You know Jake. He'll be the last to give up."

There was a long moment of silence between the two women. The clock on the living-room mantel ticked too loudly. Toby felt as stricken with loss as the first day she'd heard of the accident.

"I've got something else to tell you," Cora said, not looking up at Toby. She rubbed her forehead. "It's not good. Denise is here. She came tonight. I don't know how long she intends to stay, but she brought enough luggage for three women. She's staying in the other guest room.''

The announcement jarred Toby so deeply her fatigue and unhappiness fled in a wave of shock. She sat down dazedly. So Denise was here, tonight, under this very roof.

Cora still did not meet Toby's eyes. ''She's come back for him, all right,'' she said grimly. ''I always wanted him to get married—have a family of his own. But not with her. Dear heaven, not her. She's nothing but a beautiful blond... vampire. I didn't trust her from the first time Raynor brought her home. But Jake's never tolerated a word spoken against her. Never.''

Toby said nothing. Cora looked up at her and almost smiled. ''You know,'' she admitted, shaking her head, ''I hoped he might fall for you. You'd be perfect for him. But that would be asking for things to go right for a change, wouldn't it?''

''He's not for me,'' Toby replied, trying to sound light. ''I've done my best to be impervious to his charm.''

That was true. She simply couldn't bring herself to tell Cora how miserably she'd failed.

Cora stared off into the darkness. ''You haven't exactly seen him at his best, I know,'' she said moodily. ''And I'll admit it was strange the way he used you yesterday...to fend off those women and give Denise a jolt. I saw her face when the two of you rode off. She looked sick with jealousy. Positively sick. Not that she doesn't deserve a comeuppance. But it's not like Jake to be vengeful. At least, it didn't used to be. He's changing. Everything that's happened has changed him.''

''It'd change most people,'' Toby said softly, hoping the words held some comfort, however slight.

''Tonight they sat on the patio, talking. Just talking. But she devours him with her eyes. I couldn't watch.'' Cora sounded defeated, drained. ''Oh, he's still playing it a little cool. He'll make her pay. But she'll get him back. And I can't bear to see it."

The words froze Toby's heart. But she tried to keep her chin high. She stood, went to Cora and patted her shoulder. She tried to sound braver than she felt. "What will be, will be, Cora. You should go to bed. Worry won't help anyone—least of all you."

"That's what Herbert says." Cora groaned, rising from the chair. "And he's right. As usual. Bless him."

They exchanged good nights and parted. But Toby slept fitfully. She did not know which news hurt more: that Jake's hand would remain useless—or that in his darkest hour, he had turned not to Toby, but to Denise, the woman he had loved so tortuously and so long.

MONDAY STRETCHED out hellishly. Denise's presence permeated the house like a subtle poison. Toby, tired and frustrated, had yet to see her and didn't want to. Cora stalked about in silence, anger warring with resignation in her face. Hyde-Crippen had one of the world's most monumental hangovers, but claimed his illness was due to eating a plate of tainted bean sprouts in Sioux City.

Jake was worst of all. He looked terrible, Toby thought, as if pain and sleeplessness had made him nearly haggard. The blue eyes were shadowed and brooding. Although his cast was off, he still wore the black glove on his right hand, and he absently massaged the biceps of his right arm, as it if tormented him more than usual.

Most upsetting, he hardly bothered to speak to her. He made suggestions in clipped monosyllables. She found, perversely, she actually missed his barrage of criticism. It always maddened her, but at least she learned from it, and it was better than this cold wall of silence.

At lunchtime, he went off as usual with Hyde-Crippen. Toby and Cora ate a desultory meal in the kitchen. Toby finally had a glimpse of Denise, who'd obviously just arisen and was lovely in studied dishabille. She sat alone at the huge dining-room table, looking lonely yet proud, nibbling at strawberries and sipping champagne. She stared pensively out the picture windows toward Hyde-Crippen's quarters.

"I suppose her eating alone in the dining room is supposed to emphasize that we're the hired help." Cora sniffed. "Well, she could put on some clothes to do it. What do you call that black thing she's got on?"

"A peignoir," Toby ventured. "An expensive one."

"Looks like the best in tasteful bawdy-house wear to me," muttered Cora. "Her approach is not what I call subtle."

Jake spent an inordinately long time with Hyde-Crippen. Toby, restless, wandered back to the studio. To do so, she had to pass Denise, who now stood by the picture window. The sumptuous black lace of the peignoir made her look paler and more dramatic than ever. Denise stared down at the river, her face pensive.

Suddenly she turned and looked Toby over, very carefully.

Don't worry, Toby thought, resentful under that appraising gaze. *It's no contest, Denise. Any man who'd choose me over you is obviously deranged.*

Denise's wealth of platinum hair fell in calculated disarray down her back. Toby's dark curls were already rebelling against the silver clip that held them captive. Denise's makeup was complete and perfect. Toby wore none except a dash of pink lipstick—and she had an ink smudge on her cheek and another on her index finger. Denise looked willowy in flowing black. Toby wore jeans, her pink jogging shoes and an oversize pink T-shirt with a picture of Daisy Duck on the chest.

"So," Denise said at last. There was sadness in the set of her beautiful mouth. "So," she repeated. "You're the little thing he has living here."

Well, Toby thought bitterly, that, of course, was how
Denise would view her presence and how Jake would want
her to view it.

"I'm Toby Moranti." She approached the other woman,
stretching out her hand in greeting. "I'm Mr. Ulrick's assistant. I'm overpaid but overworked, so it comes out even.
He's with his doctor right now. You might as well sit back
down and make yourself comfortable."

Denise eyed Toby's ink-stained hand dubiously before
taking it in her own. "So..." Pain trembled in her voice.
"You're the one he's using." She squeezed Toby's hand intimately, as if the two of them were united in some deep and
bizarre way.

Toby stiffened. Denise stared down at her, radiating an
aura of brave sadness. "Jake didn't used to be cruel," Denise said softly. "Especially to me." She released Toby's
hand and paced the length of the large room. She carried
herself like a queen who has agreed to do a period of pen-
ance. If Jake was making Denise atone for her sins, he was
using Toby as an instrument of punishment, and she hated
it.

Denise's words rang in her ears: *So you're the one he's
using.* She did not try to make a graceful exit. She fled, heart
pounding rebelliously, to the sanctuary of the studio.

When Jake returned at last, he was as uncommunicative
as he'd been in the morning. He was cold, totally self-
contained.

Yet sometimes, she found him staring at her. The startling energy of the gaze from his weary face confused her.

"What's wrong?" she asked finally, uncomfortable under his disturbing scrutiny. She studied her drawings desperately. "What have I done wrong? Stop staring. Just tell
me, for heaven's sake."

As usual, he turned from her. "Nothing's wrong, Moranti," he said quietly. "You're by God perfect. Nothing
wrong at all. Just keep drawing."

He didn't have to be sarcastic, she thought darkly.

Then he became restless. Just as Toby feared, he pored over her day's work looking for errors. But he said nothing. He stood examining the panels, the same tired intensity in his eyes. He kept rubbing his arm.

She was grateful when he broke off work relatively early, before nine o'clock. But instead of going to see Denise, he went outside, alone in the moonlight. A few moments later, Toby heard Tango's nicker from the cliffs.

What is he doing to himself? she asked the darkness. *To all of them? And why? Was it the return of Denise, or the growing certainty of Hyde-Crippen's failure? Or a combination of both and all that had gone before?*

She went to her room and dressed for bed. She stared down pensively from her tower window. Denise stood on the patio, wearing a caftan that looked golden in the glow of the patio torches. The night wind tossed the wealth of her pale hair.

Toby turned away. She shouldn't care, she warned herself, lying down dispiritedly on the huge bed. She shouldn't waste an iota of time thinking of either Jake or Denise. She should worry about her own emotional survival. But always, even in her restless dreams, her mind returned to that handsome, stoic, contrary blond man, her concern for his future, his happiness.

Tuesday seemed destined to be a replay of Monday's horrors. Hyde-Crippen, recovered from his hangover, was compulsively talkative. He chattered without ceasing about Jake's progress. There was an almost crazed desperation in his babble.

Cora was right, Toby thought bleakly. Hyde-Crippen knew it was over. He had failed and was about to find himself out on the street again. He was making one last effort to pretend everything was all right.

Cora was so disgusted by the doctor and the haunting presence of Denise, she retreated completely into silence.

She roamed the house restlessly, abandoning one task for another, never finishing anything. For the first time since Toby had arrived, she burned breakfast. Fortunately, Denise did not appear for the ruined meal. She was probably still asleep, Toby thought uncharitably, having spent a long night offering Jake physical proof of just how much she still loved him.

Jake, silent and unreadable as the day before, seemed scarcely to notice Toby in the studio that morning. He sat frowning at an old manual typewriter. With his usual ferocious concentration, he used his left hand to peck out his next batch of story lines. When he wasn't typing, he rubbed his elbow. His face seemed more intent, more drawn than yesterday. Toby wondered in despair just what last-minute experiments the panicky Hyde-Crippen was performing. Cora was right—everything was going wrong at once.

At lunchtime, Jake disappeared for yet another torture session with Hyde-Crippen. Denise, fully clothed for a change, took her meal alone in the dining room. Cora scowled at the snobbery of it, and Toby shrugged philosophically. When Jake didn't return at the usual time, she helped Cora peel potatoes for the evening's supper. Still he did not come, so she and Cora sat down for an additional cup of coffee.

With Jake over half an hour late, Denise grew tired of waiting, even in the sanctuary of the socially superior dining room. She pushed open the kitchen door, impatience straining her delicate features. "Cora," she ordered, her voice shaking. "Go find Jake. I need him." In spite of her imperious tone, there was something hunted about her, a desperate helplessness.

"He's with his doctor," Cora said with false amiability. "A charming man with whom I'm sure you'd have loads in common."

"Well, get him," Denise commanded sharply, as if she were at the edge of tears. At that moment the back door opened and Jake entered. Whatever Hyde-Crippen had put him through was strenuous. A patina of perspiration gilded his features, and his gold-streaked hair hung over his forehead. His blue work shirt was damp and clung to his wide shoulders. He was rubbing his wrist again, right above the black leather glove.

He stopped momentarily in the doorway. He gave Denise a long, measuring stare. Toby felt the scene was charged with emotions she couldn't begin to understand.

"I need to talk to you." Denise's voice was small and supplicating.

He arched a brow. "I told you when you came," he answered coldly, "you'd get my nights, not my days. You said it'd be enough. It's going to have to be."

He cast a bored glance at Toby, who stood clenching and unclenching her fists. "Come on, Moranti." He nodded toward the studio. "Back to the salt mine. What are you standing there staring for? I said, back to work."

Denise watched them, her face beautiful and stricken. Although Toby disliked her, she felt an unexpected twinge of pity. If Jake intended to make Denise suffer, he was doing an excellent job.

Lips clamped grimly, Toby followed him to the studio. He seemed even less interested in her than in Denise. She was glad he didn't speak for she didn't trust herself to answer him.

Wordlessly, he examined her drawings. With a few curt recommendations for revisions, he gave them back to her. He paced. He worked at the typewriter again. He sat, taut and uneasy, studying old strips and rubbing his elbow.

From time to time, she would look up to find his eyes on her. It made her nerves tingle uncomfortably. She always looked away immediately, disconcerted, her heart flying into a broken rhythm.

Why did he look at her like that, she wondered desperately, when Denise was in the house? Or did he look at her like that because Denise was in the house? Toby gritted her teeth and tried to concentrate on work.

She broke for supper, but he did not. He didn't leave the studio. Toby and Cora dined morosely with the chatty, slightly manic Dr. Hyde-Crippen. Denise, Cora informed Toby archly, had a headache and was having supper on a tray in her room, along with a pitcher of martinis.

What was going on? Toby thought in perplexed misery as she returned to the studio. How much punishment did Jake intend to inflict on Denise, and for how long? She vowed to stay out of whatever was going on between them. Neither would she give Jake the satisfaction of showing him her own anger and frustration.

Her resolve grew thinner as the evening wore on. Darkness thickened then fell, and the night stretched around them like a desert. Why wasn't he going to her? Toby thought nervously. What was he up to?

Silently, she offered to show him her latest finished drawings. He refused to glance at them. But a few moments later, she found his bewildering gaze trained on her. He was watching her as closely as a cat does an unsuspecting mouse.

"What's wrong with you?" she asked, her fragile self-control cracking. "Why are you so quiet? Why aren't you criticising me? And why do you keep staring at me like that?"

He rubbed his elbow. He shrugged. He kept his eyes trained on hers. "Maybe I'm wondering what's wrong with you," he said sardonically.

"Me?" she asked in disbelief. "Nothing's the matter with me. You're the one who drifts around here like a ghost out of the lost legion of the damned."

He favored her with one of his cold smiles. "Is that how you see me? One of the legion of the damned? Melodramatic. But I like it."

"I don't see you any particular way," she returned defensively. She turned back to her drawing. "You've just been different lately, that's all—and you should go to your guest. She's waiting. You're remarkably rude to her."

"My 'guest' can wait. I intend to make her wait. If she finds it rude—tough. And I'm not the only one around here who's *different* lately. You're different yourself." He rose from the typing table. He stood behind her. He put his hand on the back of her neck in the old intimate gesture, and she stiffened, knowing exactly how powerfully his touch affected her.

"We've never actually been friends, Toby," he murmured. "Lately we've been close to enemies. Maybe we should go back to what we had originally. It'll be easier on everybody concerned."

And just what did we have originally? she wanted to demand. *Nothing has ever been easy between us. Nothing ever will be. The only decent thing for all concerned would be for me to leave—I should have left long ago.*

She said nothing, only sat, her pencil gripped tightly. His hand moved to her shoulder, caressing her tired muscles with sensual expertise. He bent, lifted her hair from her neck and gently kissed the nape. Shudders of pleasure and alarm trembled through her.

"Don't," she managed to say sharply. This was the same man who had told Denise his nights belonged to her, the man who pretended to want only one woman at a time, she reminded herself. She refused to let him try to make love to her when Denise was under the same roof.

"You've hired my brain and my hand," she stated coldly. "Not my emotions. And not the rest of my body. I don't play games."

She sensed him straightening behind her. His hand on her shoulder tensed, went still. "I'm tired of games myself," he returned with equal coldness. "I'd like to explain what I mean, if you'd condescend to listen."

"I'm not interested in your explanations," she muttered, and rubbed the back of her neck as if she could erase the memory of his touch. But trying to ignore him only intensified her awareness of him.

He was silent a long moment. "Fine," he snapped at last. "I see." He turned from her and went back to the typing table. He rubbed his elbow. He did not speak to her again that night.

Before bedtime, she and Cora shared a nightcap, Cora's famous coffee laced with blackberry brandy.

Toby sat back in her chair, pretending to savor her warm drink. She supposed Jake had worked late tonight to keep Denise uncertain and waiting for him. He was playing a despicable game with the two of them. She toyed with her cup and tried to keep her ragged emotions from showing.

"I've given my notice, by the way," Cora said, all too casually. "Herbert and I have been talking. Actually we've been thinking about this since before Jake's accident. It's time we got on with our own lives. He's selling the farm. He's got a buyer—AgTel, a conglomerate. We're going to tie the knot at Christmas."

Toby set down her coffee cup and for the first time in days managed a genuine smile. "Cora! That's wonderful! I'm delighted for you." Her smile faded as suddenly as it had shone. "But you won't leave Jake altogether, will you? I mean, he really couldn't function without you."

"Oh, I'll do his accounts, handle minor business, fend off the press if they get pesky," Cora said without emotion. "He can find another housekeeper—that won't be hard. Don't worry about him. It's you that you need to worry about."

"Me?" Toby asked, not comprehending. "Why me?"

"He's realized he needs you—that he's not going to do 'Heartland' without you—or somebody—not now. Maybe not ever. But—Toby—I don't think you should stay in the house after I'm gone. It won't look proper."

"I suppose not." Toby gazed into the black depths of her coffee. Christmas seemed a long way off—an eternity almost.

"Another thing is Denise," Cora cautioned. "If she comes back permanently, she probably won't want you around. She always did want to be the queen bee. Do you understand what I'm trying to say?"

"That I'm certainly going to be looking for another place to live, and that I'm probably going to be looking for another job," she replied gloomily.

"She couldn't handle having you around all the time. Look how she acts now and she's only a guest. She has to be the center of attention, and Jake knows it. He isn't easily pushed around, and he knows how good you are, but—well, she'd try to make your life miserable—"

Just what I need, Toby thought hopelessly. *Somebody else making my life miserable.* But she managed to give Cora a thumbs-up sign and a smile. "All that's still in the maybe stage—what's certain is that you and Herbert have finally set the date. So let's look on the happy side and drink to that, okay?"

She touched her cup to Cora's in salutation.

"Whatever happens," Cora said, managing to smile, "I'll miss you. Stay in touch, *kola.* You have *Wakon Tonka* in you."

"And what's that mean?" Toby asked, looking fondly at her.

"It means I don't want you to become a stranger, little friend. You have the great spirit of giving in you. A brave and selfless heart."

Toby was almost too touched to speak. "You, too," she whispered. Then, hurriedly, she said good night and excused herself. She had a choking sensation in her throat as she climbed the stairs.

It was starting to end, she told herself with foreboding. The whole thing was starting to end now. Soon Cora would be gone, and she would be gone, and it would be as if she'd never come here at all.

Then she would be safe, she told herself. She should be happy, but she was not. It was too late to be safe. No matter where she went, part of her would stay forever by this river and with the man whose eyes shone as hot and blue as the Nebraska summer sky.

She opened the door. She stopped in midstep, overcome with surprise. Denise sat on the edge of Toby's bed. The blond woman wore a black silk lounging gown that emphasized her almost otherworldly beauty. The expensive scent of her perfume filled the room.

"Hello," she said, her voice husky with suppressed emotion. Her lovely eyes flashed an unhappy challenge.

"Hello," Toby returned, not moving. Her body tensed. She felt threatened.

Denise swallowed hard, then ran her fingers through the thickness of her fair hair. "I just want you to know," she said, her voice catching slightly, "that Jake's using you. To punish me. You know that, don't you?"

"I know it perfectly well," Toby answered, holding her head higher.

"He wants me to think he's—attracted to you," Denise said. She sounded tremulous, like someone trying to be courageous. "That he's not as certain he loves me as he used to be. But he does love me. He always has." She paused for effect. "He always will."

"I'm sure," Toby said stiffly. She didn't doubt it. There was something almost hypnotic about the woman, and her beauty, her feminine vulnerability, increased it a hundredfold.

"He wants to hurt me. I can't blame him. And he's succeeded very well. Don't let him hurt you, too."

"Don't worry," Toby returned with false crispness.

"He and I—" Denise made a strange, helpless gesture—"go back further than you can imagine. Maybe to the beginning of time. We've fought it, and still fight it, but we're—'' she seemed to struggle for the precise word ''—we're destined. Destined. Do you understand?''

''Perfectly,'' said Toby, her back rigid, her hand still on the knob.

Denise nodded with satisfaction. ''Good,'' she breathed. ''Good. You see, Jake and I, no matter what we've done, we can't escape each other. We're inextricably bound. Forever. It's always been that way. It always will. I'm going to him now. I thought you should know.''

She rose and drifted past Toby like a beautiful silvery ghost. She stopped in the hallway. ''Destined,'' she said again in her husky voice. Then she moved with eerie grace toward the other tower room, Jake's room.

Toby stepped inside her room and pulled the door shut behind her. ''Destined,'' she repeated bitterly. She flung herself down on her bed and buried her face in her pillow. She made a small choking noise that she supposed was the sound of hope dying forever.

THE NEXT MORNING in the studio, she had nothing to say to Jake, nor he to her. They worked like two automatons programmed to ignore each other.

He had been rubbing his wrist this morning, and seemed more preoccupied than usual.

He went for his noon session with Hyde-Crippen his face set and hard. She wondered, distractedly, how long the doctor would remain. Jake's pain, instead of lessening, seemed to grow day by day. Absurdly, in spite of all he'd done, she felt a wave of sympathy for him.

Toby sat at the kitchen table, too depressed by her conversation with Denise the night before to eat or talk. Cora watched her with concern. Denise was nowhere to be seen. She was no doubt sleeping late again after a night of obsessive passion, Toby thought unhappily. A night of *destined* passion.

But shortly after one, Denise wafted into the kitchen with her usual ethereal air. "Where's Jake?" she demanded, her lovely face looking stricken again.

"With the doctor," Cora said shortly, clearing the table. "Do you want breakfast? Lunch?"

"No," Denise said distractedly. "Just get Jake. I need Jake."

Cora gave her a measuring glance. "Jake shows up when he feels like it." She went back to her work. "Do you want to wait in the dining room?"

"I'll wait here," Denise said, her voice small and breathy. "He comes in this way, doesn't he?"

Cora nodded.

Toby tried not to look at Denise, but the woman was hard to ignore. She was dressed in an ivory silk pant outfit with lace insets. She looked prepared to go somewhere. Diamonds glittered at her ears, and her hair shone with brilliance. Yet there was something fragile and delicate about her. Toby thought with a sinking heart that men would always want to take care of a woman like Denise.

Jake came into the kitchen, cast all three women a cold look and stopped by Toby's chair.

"Jake—" Denise's husky voice quivered. "We have to talk. Last night—"

"I gave you what you needed, Denise," he said almost brutally. "This is the cold light of day. I have work to do. Come on, love."

Before Toby realized what he was doing, Jake had pulled her chair out and helped her to her feet. He put his good arm companionably around her shoulders, and drawing her close, walked her out the kitchen door and toward the studio. Behind them Denise paled, and pain filled her violet eyes.

Toby was too shocked to speak until the studio door closed behind them. Then she ducked from beneath Jake's arm and shot an angry glance up at him. "That was rude," she said. "It was worse than rude. It was deceitful and cruel."

"Oh?" he asked, his coolness equal to her fire. "What's deceitful and cruel about it?"

"Just stop it," Toby ordered, her skin tingling where his arm had touched her. "I told you. I don't play games. I won't help you play yours. Use somebody else to punish your ladylove."

"Who's punishing her?" he asked, his voice bored, but his eyes unreadable.

"You," she returned hotly. "Cora told me what happened. How you were engaged to her and she broke it off. Well, she's beautiful. She's more than beautiful. But I don't think it's very nice that you want to make her absolutely crawl back. I think it's vile."

"I told Cora not to go gabbing about my private life," he said angrily. "For one thing, she doesn't know as much as she thinks. And I'm vile?" he mocked.

"Yes, vile," Toby practically spat. "Using me against her that way. I know she spent last night with you—and the nights before that—then you treat her like this. She knows you're trying to get even with her. She told me. You're worse than vile."

He gave her a scathing look and shook his head. "If you believe anything Denise says, you're not too bright. Stop being a prig. I like you better when you're high-handed and uppity and mean yourself."

"Oh, be sensible," Toby retorted. "I'm never high-handed and uppity and mean. But I should be. It's what you need—a taste of your own medicine."

He cocked an admonitory brow at her. "A taste of my own medicine? Fair enough. But do I have to gag it down in front of the whole nation? The entire country?"

Toby blinked in confusion. "What do you mean?" she asked.

"I mean this," he said, taking a sheet of paper from his shirt pocket and tossing it on the drawing table beside her. "You haven't been reading your mail lately, have you?"

Puzzled, Toby took up the paper and unfolded it, giving Jake a suspicious glance. Then she looked at the page, went pale and swallowed hard.

She stared at a Xerox copy of her caricature of Jake called "The Artist and His Ego." The free, nervous lines of the drawing were bolder than she remembered, the likeness to Jake more evilly accurate. The drawing of the overfed pet Ego, swollen, stupid and smug by its owner's side, made her blush scarlet.

"Wh-where did you get this?" she asked, her voice tiny with humiliation.

"It came today. From the art editor of *City Lights*," Jake said, his mouth slanted but unamused. "An old friend of mine. Read the note."

Scribbled at the bottom of the drawing was a message:

Ulrick,
This kid's address tells me he's got to be your new assistant. The drawing tells me that he's got your number. The talent tells me you'd better keep an eye on him—the kid's got what it takes. Be prepared when this hits the stands in November. (Knowing you, you probably asked for this.)
Enviously Anyway,
Ted.

Toby looked up fearfully. "I don't understand," she said. She swallowed hard again.

"I said," he gibed, "you obviously haven't been looking at your mail. Or Cora, off in space, forgot to give it to you. This probably arrived for you Saturday, when we were having such fun at Founder's Day." He reached into his hip pocket and handed her a slender envelope.

"I still don't understand," she said, shaking her head.

"Toby," he said impatiently. "A skinny envelope from a publisher usually means one thing—they've bought something from you. What they bought is that hatchet job you did on me and my poor ego."

"It can't be," she said, torn between exultation and embarrassment. She ripped the envelope open, and to her amazement, a check fell out. She unfolded a letter. They had accepted all the drawings. The first would appear in the November issue of *City Lights*.

Numbly, she bent and picked up the check. She didn't even look at the amount. It didn't matter. What mattered was that her art had been good enough to be accepted by the best. But what also mattered was that it was art done in resentment and anger. She had sold Jake out. She had loved him so much that she had to strike back at him when he'd hurt her. And she had sold him out.

"I'm sorry," she said weakly. "I did it in—a bad mood," she finished lamely. Then a light of hope came into her eyes. "I don't have to accept the money. I can tell them I won't sell. I really don't have to let them—"

"You idiot!" Jake exploded, taking the check and letter from her and slapping them on the drawing table. "Don't you understand? You made it, Toby. Not with a strip, but as a spot artist—a cartoonist's cartoonist—and for the best magazine in the States."

Toby hardly heard him. "I'll send the check back," she fretted. "I'll tell them it's all a mistake."

"You'll do no such thing," he commanded. "Good Lord, Toby, do you think my feelings are hurt? I've spent my life making fun of other people's foibles. Why should I care if somebody makes fun of mine? What's important is the style of this drawing—it's got everything you've got to give, not only the technical mastery, but the spontaneity, the clarity of vision—and that passion I've been hunting for so long."

She looked up at him in disbelief. "You mean you're not angry?"

"Do I have to climb on top of the house and yell it?" he asked, stepping closer and putting his hand on her nape under the fall of her dark curls. "I'm proud of you, Toby. Prouder than if I'd done it myself."

"But—" she began, her eyes swimming with happy tears.

"No buts," he corrected. "The other night I said some devastating things about that 'Taffy' business. I said them because they needed saying. I've regretted it ever since, because the look in your eyes was terrible, as if I'd killed something inside you. But it was only because I wanted something better to come to life—the something that shows in this drawing. You've got talent, Toby. Almost too much. It took you a long time to find which part was yours and yours alone. Do you think I give a damn if you used me for a target? I deserved it, if anybody ever did."

"You really don't care?" she asked, caught between crying and laughing.

"I care about you," he said, and bent above her. For a moment, his lips hovered provocatively near, and then they took hers. Happily, she gave herself to his kiss, winding her arms around his neck as if she could merge with him, and they could truly become one.

"See?" he asked softly, his mouth next to hers. "That passion is there. And the courage is coming along. I still want you, Toby. I can feel the passion in you right now— like a current, sweeping through you like the river. Will you admit what you're feeling? We're long overdue, Toby. I want to make love to you."

Her whole body stiffened. Her arms went wooden around his neck. She was conscious of the hardness of his chest pressed against her breasts and of how wrong that touch was. She felt suddenly cold and sick. The floor seemed to pitch beneath her feet, the air go dark. For a split second she thought crazily, *I'm back in the fun house.*

He sensed the icy tension that gripped her and studied her face, a frown forming between his brows. "We both want it," he said gruffly. "So why don't we just stop denying our feelings and get on with it?"

She dropped her arms from around his neck as if she'd been stung. She stepped back from his embrace so quickly she eluded him. "I just don't understand you," she whispered, shaking her head. "I've heard about men like you, but I never really believed—"

"Believed what?" he interrupted, his frown more intense. "You know, Moranti, I don't understand you. You go hot and cold faster than any woman I ever met. Two minutes ago you were apologizing like crazy, one minute ago you were kissing me, and now you're looking at me like I'm the Marquis de Sade."

"The Marquis de Sade was a pussycat compared to you," she retorted, almost in tears again. "Why are you doing this to me? Why are you keeping me on as your assistant—because you know Hyde-Crippen can't help you a bit? Or to torture your lady friend? Or do you just get your thrills by getting two women into your house trying to pit them against each other?"

"I don't have any ulterior motives," he shot back, then swore. "And don't call Denise my lady friend. She isn't a lady, and she's no friend. Don't tell me the green-eyed monster really has you, Toby, because if it does, it's squeezed you so tight you can't see straight."

"I see straight enough to know I'm not having any part of this," she insisted. She tossed her head so spiritedly that the clip fell from her hair to the carpet. Her curls tumbled down to her shoulders and around her face. She brushed them back impatiently. "I won't be manipulated," she stated with passion. "I won't be used—just because you can't stand needing help, and you have to put me in my place. I won't be played against some other woman, and I won't let you try to seduce me—because it's demeaning and sly and sick.''

"Demeaning?" he countered, his eyes flashing dangerously. "Sly? *Sick?* I don't believe this."

"Believe it," she admonished. "Because I'm quitting. I've put up with enough. I'd rather work on 'Dr. Dinsmore' for the rest of my life than put up with you another hour."

"Quit?" he roared. "You can't quit! I won't allow it."

"It's not a question of what you allow!" she parried. "I said I won't put up with you, and I won't. I repeat, I quit."

Her own eyes were flashing, her expression as wild and angry as his. Their gazes locked like those of two animals about to spring at each other's throats.

"And I say the hell you'll quit," Jake practically thundered. He smashed his right fist so hard against the oak file cabinet that the wood shivered from the impact.

"Ouch!" he said, rubbing his right hand. He glared at her even harder, since she had made him hurt himself. "If you walk out that door," he threatened, "I'll drag you back by your beautiful hair. I told you that you're mine, and I intend to keep you as long as necessary, and if that turns out to be—"

He stopped in midsentence. Silence. All anger drained from his face. He went suddenly pale. The blue eyes lost their fire and became oddly blank, like those of a man seeing a phantom.

"Toby," he almost whispered, rubbing his hand again.

She stared at him in alarm. *He's pushed himself too hard and too long,* she thought in panic. *He's getting sick or dying, and it's my fault.* She took a step toward him, her anger dissipating, fear rising.

"Toby," he said, so low she could hardly hear him. "I moved my hand. I felt it when I hit the file cabinet. I felt it. *My God.*"

He was holding his right wrist and staring down at the gloved fingers. She took another step closer, then stopped, her gaze riveted to his hand, transfixed.

"My God," he said again, his voice hoarse. "My God." The black gloved fingers moved slightly, then once more clenched into a fist. He raised his eyes to hers. He laughed in disbelief. "It hurts," he said, his voice oddly choked. "It actually hurts."

Gently she took his hand in hers. She squeezed it slightly. "Can you—feel that?" she asked, her eyes still holding his.

He gave her a lopsided smile, but it was a bit shaky. "I feel it. I don't believe it, but I do."

He leaned a bit unsteadily against the filing cabinet. Automatically, as if from old habit, he wound his left arm around her neck. He pressed his face against her hair. He laughed softly again. "It's going to work, Mona Lisa," he said in that same half-choked voice. "The hand is going to work again."

She leaned her head against his chest, so filled with pride and relief she wasn't sure her knees could support her weight. She kept her gentle hold on the hand as it slowly clenched and unclenched. She couldn't stop the tears this time. "You're going to be all right," she said. She pressed her face against his shirtfront, closing her eyes. "You're going to be fine."

All right, she thought. *I love you. I admit it. You win. I just can't help it.*

He lifted the gloved hand and gently stroked her cheek with the knuckles. She held it against her face, turning slightly so she could press her lips against his scarred wrist. He bent and kissed the back of her neck. He laughed again, gently.

"Look," he said, excitement rising in his voice, "go get Cora. Get Hyde-Crippen. Now. Hurry."

She didn't want to leave him, but she put her arms around him, gave him an impassioned hug, then ran for the door. "Cora!" she cried as loudly as she could. "Cora!"

She was not surprised that Denise was the first person she saw. The tall blonde stood in the living room, studying the river view. She looked at Toby with bored resentment. The sadness in her eyes was gone, replaced by a self-absorbed petulance. "What's happened?" she asked silkily. "Has he actually proposed to you? Congratulations. He has heaps of money and the house is quite nice. But you'll live the rest of your life by this muddy river. I always secretly hated it myself. It bores me to death. To death."

Toby hardly heard her. She ran into the kitchen, calling for Cora and for Hyde-Crippen.

At last she found them in the backyard. Hyde-Crippen was sunning in his baggy shorts again, the zinc oxide spread on his nose. Cora, looking semicheerful for the first time in days, was walking toward the house. She was spanking her hands together as if cleaning them of something unpleasant.

"It's Jake," Toby said to both of them at once. "It's his hand. He can move it. He has feeling in it."

Cora looked at her an instant. Her mouth opened in surprise. Then she began to race toward the house with surprising swiftness, even for Cora.

Hyde-Crippen sat up, but didn't move. He looked stunned. Toby went up to him and put her hand on his round, sweaty little shoulder. She swallowed hard. "You did it." She bit her lip. "I owe you an apology. Both Cora and I do. I'm sorry I doubted you. You did it. Thank you."

Still the little man said nothing. Toby looked down. To her amazement and embarrassment she saw that he seemed to be crying. He whipped his cheap sunglasses off and rubbed away the tears with his fists, like a little boy. "It worked," he said. "I believed for so long it would. But nobody else did. Except Mr. Ulrick—and he'd almost given up."

"Come on, Doctor," Toby said, patting him awkwardly. "You can see for yourself." She took a tissue from the pocket of her jeans and gave it to him. She looked away in embarrassment as he blew his nose and wiped his eyes. He was so overcome that he leaned on her weakly all the way back to the studio, chattering wildly.

"All my life I've wanted to be important," he babbled in a mixture of pride and confession. His spurious English accent had disappeared and his voice sounded suspiciously as if he, too, had come from New Jersey. "All my life there's been only one good thing about me—that I loved knowledge. I realize I'm a weak man in many ways—and that the first impulse of people is to laugh at me. But I've loved science and tried to extend its boundaries. I've often pretended to be what I am not. But at last I've proved what I can be—a man of medicine. A pioneer. A scientist."

They found Jake in the studio, grinning as he tried to extricate himself from Cora's bear hug. He extended his right hand to Hyde-Crippen with the admonition not to squeeze too hard, it still hurt.

"Best sign in the world," the little man chirped, stripping off the glove and examining the fingers. He kept shaking his head in wonder.

"Come here, you little scalawag," Cora ordered, swooping down on Hyde-Crippen. Like Jake, he was the recipient of one of her ferocious hugs. "I misjudged, I insulted you and I reviled you," Cora said, squeezing the little man until his eyes bugged. "But, sweetheart, I love you. You are a bonafide genius."

"Stop hugging him, Cora," Jake smiled. "If you really love him get him a drink—and a cigar. There are some Havanas in the humidor."

"Oh, no," Hyde-Crippen protested. "I don't drink. I certainly don't smoke. It would be—"

"You don't have to pretend any more, Doc," Jake said. "You've proved yourself. So be yourself. Cora—give him the best bourbon."

"Well," Hyde-Crippen said obligingly, "if you insist. I'll have to examine you more thoroughly later, but perhaps a bit of celebration is in order...."

"Come on," Cora said, practically jerking the little man behind her. "I'm going to personally pour your bourbon, and personally light your cigar, and call up Herbert and tell him to come over, so he can see me personally eat my words in front of you."

Jake smiled after them. He walked toward Toby and again he put his left arm around her neck in the old intimate gesture. "Ever think you'd see that?" he asked, looking down at her fondly. "Cora practically kissing Hyde-Crippen?"

"No," she replied happily, looking back at him.

He leaned down and kissed her, first on the nose, then full on the lips. Blissfully, she let him.

"Now," he said, straightening up and tucking one of her curls behind her ear. "Where were we? Oh, yes. You were going to walk out. I was going to drag you back by the hair. It was a devil of a fight. Do you suppose we can get the mood back?"

She sobered suddenly. He had her, as usual, precisely where he wanted her. "I don't want to get the mood back," she admitted.

"Me either," he said. "I don't want you to leave. I won't let you."

She resisted the desire to sink back against him, to rest her head against his chest once more. "I have to go, Jake," she said softly. She did not struggle against his embracing arm, but she could not yield to it either. "You won't need me much longer anyway. You'll be able to work on your own again. And I can't stay in the same house with Denise. It isn't right. And it isn't fair."

"I do need you—I already told you that. Who knows how long I'll need you? I'm starting to think it's forever. And Denise who?"

She shrugged unhappily, not wanting to look at him. "You know perfectly well," she said. "She's in love with you. And you never stopped loving her—even if you want to hurt her before you take her back."

He forced her to turn to face him. He tipped her chin up. With his ungloved right hand he softly touched her lips. "She was never in love with me. Once I thought I was in love with her. It's hard to explain, Toby, but what existed between Denise and me wasn't healthy. Maybe she really did love my brother. I don't know. I doubt if she knows. When he died, we clung to each other. Then she tried to use me as a substitute for him, as if she could pretend he'd never died. I—I thought I owed it to Raynor to take care of her. And she was so beautiful, and so vulnerable. But—" He struggled for words, his face working with emotion that he had kept long-contained.

"But?" Toby probed softly, because she felt at long last that Jake was letting her proceed beyond the formidable barrier of his self-imposed privacy.

"It isn't easy to say, Toby," he finally continued. "I was too young then to know that vulnerability can be the strongest of weapons. When Rayn was alive Denise manipulated us against each other. We both wanted to take care of her. She was that kind of girl. She had some kind of breakdown when Rayn died. I didn't understand it then. I only knew I had to take care of her. I found out that whatever I did, how much attention I gave her, it wasn't enough. She wanted more. She needed more."

He sighed wearily. "Then the manipulations began in earnest. She'd tell me she didn't love me—she'd always love Raynor. I'd be confused and, I'll admit it, hurt. Then she'd turn around and say no, it had always been me she'd loved, never Raynor, and she felt guilty about Raynor's death. It got crazy. I didn't tell Cora. I didn't tell anybody. It didn't seem fair to Raynor to expose her. But I began to realize that Denise was very sick. But I still felt responsible for her, because of Rayn mostly.''

"Then you haven't been in love with her all these years?" Toby asked incredulously.

He laughed bitterly. "No, but I've remembered her. Oh, God how I've remembered her. I fell out of love with her years ago, about the third time she said she was going to leave her husband for me. You know who she threw me over for? This is a good one—it could go into a comic strip. Her psychiatrist, that's who. She was so good at what she did, she even pulled him into her private circus. Cora doesn't know that, either. She thinks Denise married some doctor for money. She didn't. She married for power. Then she had a beautiful three-way game going: she really loved me. She really loved Raynor. She really loved her husband. What I finally realized was Denise never loved anybody except herself. This isn't the first time she'd left her husband or tried to play me against him. But it's the boldest, and it better be the last. Because this time I showed her what she thought she'd never see—a woman I loved more than I ever thought I loved her.''

"What?" Toby said in a small voice. She had let his arm enfold her now and sank helplessly against it, looking up at him.

"I didn't want to hurt her. I just wanted her to drop me from that sad old game. I finally had to tell her to go home. I'm through with her machinations. She's leaving, Toby."

She shook her head, keeping her eyes on his solemn blue ones. "She can't be. She just got here," she replied.

"She insisted on coming," Jake said, tracing the outline of her upper lip. "She wouldn't take no for an answer. Maybe she had to see I meant what I said. When she got here, to the house, she realized I'd found somebody else. I tried to tell her nicely at first. Last night I told her in no uncertain terms. It finally got through to her. I told Cora to load her bags back into her car. She should be on her way home now. To her husband. Heaven help him."

She looked up at him, her dark eyes uncertain.

"I told her that day in the park, Toby. I said I'd found someone else. At first I thought I might be lying—then, as if somebody hit me, I understood it was the truth. I knew I felt something stronger than I'd ever felt in my life. For you. Because you were so strong and real and fine."

"But—you went to her that night," she stammered. "And then she moved in—and Cora said—"

He laid his finger on her lips again. "Shh, Toby. Cora saw her fears, that's all. All I wanted to do was convince Denise she had to stop deluding herself. What happened between us is ancient history. It can't be revived. One night I rode Tango down to the river, near the place where Raynor drowned. I stayed there, a long time, looking at the stars on the water and thinking."

He framed her face with both hands, the right fluttering lightly against the line of her brow, the curve of her cheek. "I thought how Rayn wouldn't want me to go any further protecting Denise. I knew he'd understand. I thought about how much I wanted you, and how I'd done the wrong thing with you every step of the way. I thought how I'd vowed never to want anybody again, never to need anybody again, and here I was—wanting and needing you. Denise played sick power games with me and with all the men in her life. It burned me, and the worst part is that I started doing the same thing with you. I wondered what I was going to do about it. I thought if Denise saw for herself, once and for all that I was through with her, she'd go back to her husband. I'd pay off whatever last debts I owed her, for her own sake or for Raynor's. Then I could concentrate on making things up to you—and hoping you could love me back."

He put his right forefinger against her lips again. "How beautiful your mouth feels, Toby," he whispered. "How good it is to touch you with both hands. How good it is to want somebody. To need somebody. To love somebody.''

"What?'' she asked again, a shiver in her voice.

"I accused you of being a coward.'' He smiled. "But it was me. Until that moment that I stormed and raved and forbade you to go away, I didn't want to admit I adore you. Somehow you walked into my life and filled all the empty places. I want you next to me for the rest of my life. I have an irresistible urge to use words like *always* and *forever* and *eternally* around you.''

She managed to smile at him, tremulous and shy. She put her hands on his shoulders. "How do I know you don't just want an inexpensive live-in assistant?'' she asked, trying to hide her confusion in humor. "With Cora going, you may just want me to stay around to do your drawing and fix your spaghetti.''

He wound both arms around her tightly. He rubbed his chin against her hair. "Draw whatever you like,'' he said. "Work on the strip if you want—I hate to admit it, but you draw it as well as I do. Well—almost. Or draw your own things, now that you've found your own style. As for your spaghetti, I don't give a hoot about it. I want your passion, not your pasta, Mona Lisa.''

She raised on her toes, pressing closer to him. "Consider it yours,'' she said.

He laughed, kissed the tip of her nose, and hugged her more tightly. "All right, Toby. I give up. Do I have to beg you to say it?''

"Say what?'' she asked, standing a little higher on her toes, wishing he would kiss her again.

"Say that you love me. That you could put up with me— for a lifetime, maybe?''

"I love you,'' she declared. "I'd put up with you for a thousand lifetimes. A hundred thousand.''

"Then welcome," he said, his voice velvety with desire, "to the heart of the heart of the country. Oh, Toby, do you know how much I need you?"

"No," she said, "tell me."

"Better than that," he said, breathing against her lips. "I'll draw you a picture."

Harlequin Romance

Coming Next Month

2881 DREAM OF LOVE Kay Clifford
Posing as her film star boss's fiancée, Melissa accompanies him to
California. It is a position she finds difficult to explain when she
meets and falls in love with another man!

2882 NIGHT OF THE SPRING MOON Virginia Hart
A young woman who returns to her Missouri hometown—and to
the man she once loved—finds herself in an emotional dilemma.
She's torn between her renewed feelings for him and loyalty to her
best friend.

2883 HIGH COUNTRY GOVERNESS Essie Summers
Sheer desperation drives New Zealand sheep station owner
Nathanial Pengelly to hire the head beautician from his father's
store as a governess. But Letty is far more than just a lovely face and
sets out to teach him an unforgettable lesson!

2884 HIDDEN DEPTHS Nicola West
Tessa doesn't expect open arms when she arrives in Arizona to
bridge years of silence between her mother and her grandfather.
But at least she intends to see him. If only her arrogant cousin will
stop acting as guardian gatekeeper!

2885 BITTER DECEPTION Gwen Westwood
Journalist Sophia, visiting the cottage she's inherited in France,
finds her neighbor, famous mountain climber Fabien de Cressac,
accessible and irresistible—so she interviews him. As love grows
between them, however, she realizes the published story will end
their relationship....

2886 TO TAME A WILD HEART Quinn Wilder
Guide Chance Cody has no use for spoiled rich brats—especially
Aurora Fairhurst who's joined his wilderness trek to escape an
arranged marriage. Not until Aurora finds a new honest self, does
she find the way to his heart.

Available in January wherever paperback books are sold, or
through Harlequin Reader Service.

In the U.S.
901 Fuhrmann Blvd.
P.O. Box 1397
Buffalo, N.Y. 14240-1397

In Canada
P.O. Box 603
Fort Erie, Ontario
L2A 5X3

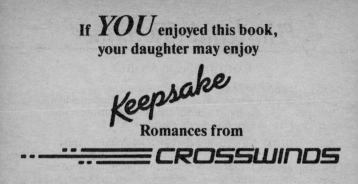